Heard Anything?

A Guide for the College-Athletic Recruiting Fan

Heard Anything?

A Guide for the College-Athletic Recruiting Fan

by Glen Waddle

Illustrated by Phil McFarland

QRP BOOKS
Brandon, Mississippi

DEDICATION

This book is dedicated to all recruiting fans who can't wait until Signing Day to find out who their team signed in the recruiting wars.

This first book is also dedicated to Chuck Rounsaville and Mac Gordon, who showed great courage and guts to ask me to write a recruiting column, and to John Hoffman, Program Director for WMC radio in Memphis, who thought enough of my voice and semi-talents to start me in the radio call-in show business in Jackson, circa summer 1984.

Thanks also to the recruiting gurus, call-in show hosts, sportswriters and recruiting fans who provided me with the experiences and information over the years to write this book.

Glen Waddle
Jackson, Mississippi

Copyright © 1993 by
Quail Ridge Press

All Rights Reserved

Manufactured in the United States of America

Library of Congress Cataloging-in-Publication Data

Waddle, Glen, 1955-
    Heard anything? : a guide for the college-athletic recruiting fan
    / by Glen Waddle : illustrated by Phil McFarland.
        p. cm.
    ISBN 0-937552-51-8 : $9.95
    1. High school athletes—Recruiting—United States. 2. College sports—United
States—Organization and Administration. I. Title.
GV350.5.W44   1993
796.071'173—dc20   93-24371
                                                             CIP

Contents

RECRUITING SERVICES CROSS REFERENCE

CHAPTER 1
Heard Anything?

WELCOME TO THE Wonderful World of Gurus and Goofiness and the Cosmos of Commitments—verbal, public or private!

Welcome to the time honored spectacle where coffee shop rumors and phone lines are filled with speculation, guesswork and tales about high school and junior college athletes and their pursuit of athletic excellence.

Welcome to a sports phenomenom where guys with names such as Emfinger, Forrest, Grosz, Lemmings, Greenberg, Duva, Terranova, and Buchalter are worshipped by the sporting masses and held in high regard for their endless ratings and "expertise" on prepsters hoping and angling for college scholarships.

And welcome to the realm of recruiting where outdated and ill-timed information is anticipated by "recruitniks" with the eagerness of the arrival of the rites of spring!

Such is the nature of writing about the most bizarre cottage industry that exists in the sports scene of the United States in any era. The business of following collegiate athletic recruiting is a multimillion dollar industry that thrives on newsletters, rating services, player lists, faxes, 900 numbers, and large doses of rumors and hearsay. There is no way to stay ahead of a lunatic fringe of recruiting followers that thrive in the Deep South.

The drudgery and annual bloodletting that is known as collegiate recruiting has been called many names, most on the side of being very uncomplimentary. They say in the South that there are four, count 'em, *four* seasons to college football—fall practice, the regular season, spring practice, and recruiting. Recruiting is considered to be the "fourth season." Many writers and media members who become inundated by recruiting phone calls and inquiries from late November to mid -February on signing day call it the "Silly Season." Being a part of this madness, I can confirm that that last title is extremely accurate.

If you outlined a "typical" year in collegiate athletic recruiting, it would go something like this:

FEBRUARY: Signing Day for football starts on the first or second Wednesday of the month. Football signings for college football last until mid-April. Dates are set by the NCAA—the National Collegiate Athletic Association.

MARCH: Spring sports begin active recruiting, plus basketball recruiting heats up. While football spring practice goes on, coaches prepare for May evaluations.

APRIL: Mid-April marks the start of signings for basketball, baseball, track ,and all other sports. Spring football practice concludes and coaches continue to prepare for May evaluations.

MAY: Basketball, baseball, track and other sports, except for football conclude signings. Football coaches are allowed to personally evaluate players at high schools, junior colleges, and community colleges across the nation. The coaches look at upcoming seniors and glance at incoming juniors. It is from these evaluations that crucial decisions are made about whom to scout in the fall.

JUNE: Football coaches attend clinics, play golf, go to alumni meetings, and consume adult beverages. Recruiting is usually in a dead period during the summer months.

JULY: More of same from July except that baseball coaches . are continually evaluating and football coaches prepare for fall practice while attending more intense alumni and media affairs. Mail-outs are sent by the schools during this time period to potential recruits. Contact is allowed by phone on a limited basis during this period.

AUGUST: Fall practice for football begins and mail-outs continue to prospective recruits. Basketball, baseball, and other sports are in their "dead" or "quiet" periods of recruiting where contact cannot be initiated with recruits.

SEPTEMBER: When the schedule gets underway, so do the "unofficial" visits. Recruits are allowed to attend campus games, and they receive complimentary tickets, meals, and athletic and academic facilities. They must pay their own way to come on campus, and the school cannot finance any special entertainment or provide housing in any way.

OCTOBER: "Unofficial" visits continue and football assistants are allowed to attend games and scout out potential signees. They are limited to a certain number of weekends to attend these games, and they cannot have any contact with recruits while attending these games. If they have "incidental" contact, they can show "normal civility" ("Hi! How ya doing?"). Basketball and baseball recruiting heat up with preparations for the "Early Signing Period."

NOVEMBER: "Unofficial" visits continue and football staffs begin to pare their recruiting lists down to about 100 or so players. Schools can only sign 25 players and they can only have 85 to 95 on a squad. Signees must meet academic requirements that combine grade point average in high school core curriculum classes and a certain mark in either the ACT or SAT standardized tests before they can sign scholarships. In mid-November, the "Early Signing Period" starts for basketball and baseball. During this one-week period, outstanding seniors can sign letters of intent early with the schools of their choice and not have to worry about scholarships during the rest of their senior year.

DECEMBER: In mid-month, junior college and community college (JUCO, for short) players can sign football letters of intent. Some JUCO players become eligible to attend class and participate in spring drills in January, while others may have to wait until next August. "Official" visits begin during this month for the high school players. On an "official" visit, the school pays for transportation, lodging, entertainment, and anything else it can get away with. Typically, the recruit visits the whole campus, tours all facilities, speaks with academic people about courses, attends a campus basketball game, sees lots of beautiful coeds, and talks with the head football coach. Current players assist the recruits as salesmen/escorts. A high school recruit is allowed to have five official visits during his recruitment, and a school is limited to sponsoring 70 official visits per recruiting period. Getting a star player to visit your campus is half the battle. Usually, if you can get someone on campus, you can sell him on your school. This is also the time of the year when the head football coach can take his *one* home visit to talk, and hopefully convince the player and his parents to sign that letter with their school. The head coach has to be accompanied by an assistant coach. This assistant is usually the position coach that needs that particular player's talents, or the coach that is recruiting that particular area. Assistant coaches divide up the state and out-of-state areas among them for recruiting trips concerning evaluations and fall game scouting. If they can't see the recruit in person, they have to evaluate by viewing film or videotape. Much of the information gathered by the assistants depends on their background, evaluation skills, and their ability to relate to the high school players.

JANUARY: "Official" visits conclude and recruiting heats up. This is the most intense month in recruiting. This is the time of the year when you read about "commitments," visits, rumors, hearsay, and other crazy stuff. January is the month when the 900 numbers, the radio sports call-in shows, and the recruiting services really earn their keep. January is also the month when the coaching staff and recruiting coordinators compile a list of outstanding juniors for high school and available JUCOs. The typical recruiting list compiled at this time may feature anywhere from 500 to 1,000 names. It is shortened after May evaluations and fall scouting to about 100 names of players the school knows it can sign.

FEBRUARY: It starts all over again after Signing Day. The never ending cycle keeps on going and going and going....

*****

To give you an idea of just how crazy southerners are about college football and basketball recruiting, this book is full of anecdotes and true stories of what goes on when colleges seek athletes for NCAA letter-of-intent signatures. Through these battle tales, some incredibly entertaining insight can be gained into the world of recruiting. Some words of warning: many of these tales outline the fringe elements that live and die by the decision of an acne-faced, strong-armed, speedy 18-year-old as to where he or she goes to college. The range and depth of collegiate recruiting "followers" is unbelievable. They are all know-

ing, all seeing, and all hearing, and they crave more "scoop" constantly.

The buzzwords for all of this are the title of this book. The most frequently repeated phrase when fans talk recruiting is: *"Have you heard anything?"* When signing day approaches, the signing buffs will cut it down to *"Heard anything?"* Most recruiting followers know exactly what this phrase means as if it is some kind of cultish password for information about recruits.

There is an excellent and true sample story about what you will find in the following chapters of this book. One January afternoon in my former law office in Jackson, Mississippi, I received a call about recruiting. On the surface, it seemed to be a call that I had answered thousands of times before in my years as recruiting columnist for the *Ole Miss Spirit*, a weekly publication devoted entirely to the University of Mississippi athletic scene, and my radio call-in shows on WSLI or WJDX radio's Sportsline, which lasted, amazingly, eight years from 1984 - 1992.

My receptionist informed me that the call was about Ole Miss recruiting, so that tipped me off that this would be your typical "Heard anything?" call. Little did I know what was on the other end. When I picked up with my standard "This is Glen Waddle, may I help you?", I heard the sputtering static of a car phone.

The caller, whose name I have forgotten for reasons to be made all too clear, said that he wanted some information on possible signees for Ole Miss, and that he was in a hurry. Since I didn't have all of my recruiting paraphernalia in front of me, I explained that I didn't have all of "my recruiting stuff" in the office, but I would try my best to answer his questions. After we chatted a bit about Mississippi recruits, the caller explained to me who he was and what he was doing.

Of all things, this guy was a Chicago heart surgeon who had graduated from Ole Miss both undergrad and medical school and was on his way to the hospital to perform emergency open heart surgery! He had called me minutes before he would attempt to save someone's life in an operating room just to talk football recruiting, because he "didn't get much Ole Miss recruiting information up North," and he "had to get a Signing Day fix."

Stunned, I gave him as much information as I had, plus the latest commitments and rumors on Ole Miss recruiting. He seemed perfectly satisified, and suddenly, he said, "I'm almost at the hospital, got to go!"

Minutes after he dashed off to scrub up and cut into someone's chest, I was still holding the other end of the phone in complete amazement. I had done hundreds of articles about recruiting, taken thousands of calls on and off the air, read thousands of recruiting updates and stories, and thought that I had seen and heard just about everything there was about the subject of college football or basketball recruiting. I was dead wrong.

Here was an upper-class, well-educated heart surgeon about to plunge a scalpel into a human body to try and save a life, and all this guy was thinking about was how Ole Miss was going to sign some 17- or 18-year-old to help them win football games years down the road!?! I decided right then and there that there was no rhyme or reason to this business of following the whimsy of high school students and where they wanted to go to get their higher educations.

Even more startling was the later revelation that other sportswriters shared the same experience, and similar incidents had happened to them. Billy Watkins of the Jackson *Clarion-Ledger* was working the sports desk on one particular signing day and was helping other writers at the *CL* gather lists of signees. Billy received a call from a local doctor who was on his way to an emergency room, but just had to know the signees for a particular school.

After Billy told the caller in so many words to "get a life," and after a short and brusque outline on the information the M.D. requested, Billy hung up and shook his head in utter disbelief. Billy now writes for the "Southern Style" features section of the *Clarion* and no longer has to fool with that type of incredible recruiting fringe element. He's out of the sports department and (Surprise! Surprise!) there is little wonder that he's better off at his new assignment.

These are the type of anecdotes that you will find throughout this book. At the end, you will read profiles and information about recruiting services from all across the U.S. The flavor of this book is distinctly southern; it will focus primarily on the South and the Southeastern Conference, without a doubt the most competitive intercollegiate athletic conference in the nation. You will read funny and sad tales, all true, about how innocent(?) prepsters are lured to sign scholarship papers with colleges and universities.

Have you ever called a 900 number to find out where a 17- or 18- year-old high school senior will be attending college? Have you ever shelled out hard-earned bucks to have some stranger out of state fax you a list of recruits to your office fax machine to find out where a group of 17- and 18-year-old football players may go for their higher education? Have you ever plunked down big bucks to have some recruiting "guru" describe how he feels about the speeds, weights, times, and attributes of these 17- and 18-year-old gridiron and hoop heroes? Have you ever called a sports radio call-in show and said *"Have you heard anything about where Billy Joe Blue Chip may be leaning?"*

If you answered yes to any of those questions or if you even thought about doing those things, then this book is your guide through the maze of college recruiting. This piece of work is devoted to the "recruitniks" and the casual observer who treats recruiting as a hobby. This written offering is for your benefit, your information, and for whatever we charged for you to take this home! This book is also a very handy guide with a glossary, reference material on recruiting services, and a full discussion of many NCAA rules and regulations average fans may encounter.

With this book, you haven't *"Heard Anything?"* until you have *"Read Everything"* in these pages. Enjoy.

CHAPTER 2

ONE-900-R-U-KIDN'?

YOU SEE ADS on television for 900 numbers constantly these days. Indeed, since the phone company created this monster known as the 900 service, more Americans have shelled out their "buck and whatever" on 900 numbers than they care to admit. The image of the 900 number service is certainly not as pure as Ivory soap. "Phone Sex" services dominate the 900 number scene almost exclusively.

Technology, they say, can be a help or a hindrance, and in the case of 900 number services, it's hard to evaluate the merit of forking over hard-earned bucks to hear some gal swoon, sigh, and breathe heavily over the telephone. With 900 numbers so closely tied to sex and pornography, it's easy to see why 900 services would be so successful with football recruiting! Sleaze does beget sleaze!

The *Ole Miss Spirit,* under the leadership of former publisher Mac Gordon and editor Chuck Rounsaville, pioneered the use of 900 numbers to provide information on recruiting. The whole thing seemed, at the time, to be so natural and innocent. Since most of the recruiting info was spread on the phone lines, and since Chuck and Mac would sit in their offices and dole it out free, why not charge for the stuff? After all, turning a profit is the American way, and the *Spirit* phone lines were going through meltdown before and after Signing Day.

In 1987, Mac and Chuck approached the athletic staff at Ole Miss about creating a 900 number service for Signing Day lists and information. If it was successful, then the service would be expanded for next year, and it would also take the heat off the athletic department telephones on Signing Day, when every Tom, Dick, and Harry

called in. This tied up phone lines when assistant coaches desperately had to stay in touch with their offices. That practice was eliminated with the creation of the NCAA's "Fax and FedEx" rule where recruits now mail, express, or fax their letters-of-intent into athletic offices.

But Mac and Chuck had tapped onto an idea that has now exploded in the world of recruiting. The present-day *Ole Miss Spirit* 900 number now services Ole Miss followers across the nation and also takes in other SEC schools for recruiting information on Signing Day. It is a tremendously profitable enterprise and easy money. It also saves the office staff ears from fielding all of those *"Heard Anything?"* calls.

In 1987, however, 900 numbers were still considered experimental. Working in conjunction with Ole Miss Sports Information Director Langston Rogers and his staff, Mac and Chuck arranged for information about Ole Miss signees to be placed into the 900 number message, and fans could simply call into that number to find out whom exactly the Rebels had signed before reading the paper the next morning. That's how addicted some recruiting junkies are in these days of impatience.

Fans were encouraged to use the 900 number, and it was faster and easier to access. Using the 900 number kept the athletic department lines free and would be a huge service to a large number of recruiting followers. Wednesday, February 11, 1987, was the target Signing Day and everything was in place.

Well.... *almost* everything was set.

The 900 number was to be turned on by the phone company early morning and was to remain on line until the end of the next day when most of the recruits had signed with Ole Miss. The *Spirit* had run the number continuously and we were beating the subject to death in columns and ads. After all, this was a big deal, a new technology, and a marvel to behold for some folks, and it had to be treated in a reverent manner.

The Jackson *Clarion-Ledger* was probably grateful that Mac, Chuck, Langston, and the Ole Miss staff had taken the time to set this whole thing up. After all, that would free up their phone lines and keep things flowing smoothly at the paper. Writers on deadline hate useless interruptions, especially when the caller at the other end is annoying them about who signed where. Unless the writers cover recruiting on a regular beat, they simply hate the calls and the topic matter. The *Clarion* gladly published the 900 Ole Miss number.

The number printed by the *Clarion*, however, was not even close to the 900 number set up by the Ole Miss contingent. They had printed the wrong number! To make matters worse, the number they had printed was to a *Penthouse* magazine sex line!

I discovered this at 7:30 A.M. on Signing Day. Curiosity drove me to call the number early to see if it was working. After all, this was something new and improved and would definitely be mentioned in my Signing Day column for the *Spirit*. When I heard that sexy, steamy female voice cooing on the other end of the phone, I knew something was dreadfully wrong. I checked the *Spirit* listed number against the *Clarion* number immediately and discovered the printing error.

After hearing that gal on the other end of the phone, I became journalistically inspired and called the news director at my station, Randy Bell of WJDX radio in Jackson. I told Randy that the *Clarion* had really screwed up, no pun intended, and that he should call the number and get it on tape. Randy jumped on the story and our general manager, Kenny Windham, even got into the act and called Paul Harvey, who added it to his widely listened to and nationally syndicated noon broadcast. Other Jackson stations and the Associated Press soon picked up on the 900 number *faux pas* and blasted it all over the place.

Next week, in their recruiting wrap-up in their college football section, the *Sporting News* devoted some space to the great 900 number mixup. Laughter could be heard clear across the South at the first attempt at 900 technology for recruiting. The *Clarion Ledger* had to perform damage control and retracted their error. The *Clarion* higher-ups issued an apology and talked about offering refunds, but that was just talk.

After word got around about the wrong number, many guys tried out the number just to hear the "message." Some callers on my special Signing Day edition of SportsLine that night commented that they had called the number "several times" just to make sure! The whole incident broke up the tension of the day and made everything light and lively—or deep and heavy if you called the *Clarion* number!

12

It was not normal to see the highly pressurized day of inking football recruits turn into one of enjoyment and guffaws. Instead of listening to a mundane list of who signed at Ole Miss from whatever high school, you heard a seductive female (we assume it was female!) proclaiming how her virtue was progressing at the moment. As I commented in the *Ole Miss Spirit*, "it's not every day you see cornpone turned into pornphone." What a hoot!

Ole Miss Coach Billy Brewer took it all in stride, and in the spirit of the moment, he cracked some great one-liners about his new "female recruits." He commented that his "newest signee had great breath control and stamina" for all the heavy breathing that she put forth on the phone. Billy was asked all the usual questions about how fast she ran the 40, her measurements, and where he would play her in the fall. The jokes lasted for days.

But 900 numbers have come a long way, baby, from the mislistings and the good natured humor in 1987. Nearly every established recruiting service has a 900 number and many athletic departments are looking at the dollar signs and convenience when it comes to the 900 numbers. The current *Spirit* 900 number has several menus for the caller to choose from, and the 900 number even updates all the latest scores and events surrounding Ole Miss athletics. Editor/Publisher Chuck Rounsaville swears by, not at, the 900 numbers. It's a pure profit type of operation, and one that is around for the long haul. Having used 900 numbers for recruiting information, I can tell you that it is a technological marvel and reaches thousands upon thousands of recruiting followers. The services and recruiting "gurus" make a living off of these things from December to mid-February.

A 900 number danger is the common occurrence of someone who doesn't know diddley about recruiting in any shape, form, or fashion. These "huckster gurus" commonly just set up a 900 number and feed false information on the line just to entice some unsuspecting recruiting fan to call in and listen to pure recruiting junk. If a 900 number is not operated by someone who also has a recruiting service with newsletters and the like, then steer clear. Also, persons or services that use a 900 number setup must, under federal communications and advertising/commerce laws, provide information up front about prices per minute and other information about the line. If the recruiting 900 number you are dialing does not provide this info, stop dialing!

So, 900 numbers are the absolute future of the business of recruiting. Without one, a service limits itself to expensive and time-consuming mail-outs and fax services. Recruiting developments happen nearly every day in December and January, and reliable services use these numbers to keep the public and subscribers current. With a 900 number, you can easily program in what you want and update on a daily or hourly basis. A list of the 900 numbers provided by recruiting services and other publications is included in this book with each service that chooses to run such a number.

Be cautious of the 900 numbers. Sometimes, in an effort to squeeze more money out of the recruiting consumer, a service will have a lengthy menu or list of schools and you will have to sit there and listen to it all before choosing a program. That simply sucks up the caller's money in large chunks and makes even more money for the service providing the 900 number. The numbers also change frequently without notice and the information, as mentioned here, is sometimes shaky at best. Much of the reliability depends on the particular service and the reputation that it carries.

ONE-900-R-U-KIDN' seems like the perfect phone number to sum up this recruiting business, doesn't it?

Recruiting in the South

If you live in the Deep South and you are any kind of a football fan, then you know and appreciate the frenzy over Signing Day and the ultimate importance of recruiting. Recruiting in the South is unlike anything anywhere in the United States. The best way to illustrate this point is to profile what goes on in a typical southern state. By examining the ins and outs of one of the Dixie states, readers can get an overall feel and indepth analysis as to why people are the way they are when it comes to following recruiting.

Since your author cut his teeth on football recruiting in the Magnolia state, this chapter will focus on the state of Mississippi. Recruiting in Mississippi is very unique since numerous colleges offer football within the state borders. In addition to the in-state schools, many other colleges from across the U.S. roam into the state looking for gridiron talent.

It would be relatively easy to talk about the top football recruit producers in America, namely, Florida, California and Texas. That's almost too easy and, to be honest, recruiting in those states is based on large populations. There are plenty of top recruits to stock college programs in these states. Viewing the state of Mississippi, on the other hand, may provide you with more entertainment value. If it doesn't, skip this chapter!

By examining the trials and tribulations of recruiting in Mississippi, however, insight into the recruiting process can be acquired. This is a highly competitive state when it comes to athletics. Rivalries are fierce to the point of the absurd and there are few recruiting plums to pick off the talent trees.

When it comes to football and basketball recruiting, the state Mississippi is the stripped-out mine you read about in environmental journals and publications. Mississippi is thinly populated, with a total number of about 2.5 million residents in the entire state. It is a state of proud traditions and outstanding athletic excellence.

Still, the in-state teams struggle to load up their programs with highly talented Mississippians. For reasons that range from TV exposure and prestige to the size of weight rooms and colors of T-shirts, Mississippi players, unless they have loyal ties to the school or if the school offers a certain curriculum, head out of state. The entire SEC recruits Mississippi heavily along with ACC powers such as Florida State, Georgia Tech, and Clemson and independents such as Tulane in New Orleans, Memphis State, and large powers such as Notre Dame, UCLA and Michigan.

Marvelously talented athletes frequently leave the state for better athletic and academic opportunites. Philadelphia's Marcus Dupree was one of the greatest running backs in the state of Mississippi, but when it came to recruiting, he chose Oklahoma. Marcus' recruiting was chronicled by noted author Willie Morris in *The Courtship of Marcus Dupree*. Noted basketball players such as Chris Jackson and Ronnie Henderson (LSU), Rodney McCray and Kenny Payne (Louisville), James Robinson & Derrick McKey (Alabama), and Othella Harrington (Georgetown) leave this state almost as soon as the offer is made. Many of these players receive intense criticism from Mississippians who desperately urge them to stay at home. Many of these same Mississippians go so far as to exert pressure, financial or otherwise, on the player and/or their parents to induce the player to play in the Magnolia State.

The home folks hold grudges against the players that leave the state. When the player signs out of state, the fans and alumni instantly put pressure on the newspapers and other media not to even mention that player's name again in any kind of context. If a hometown paper follows that player through college and the pros, Magnolia State residents continue to hound the reporters and they chastise them severely for tracing the career of a "traitor."

On top of all of this, Mississippi, per capita, produces more football players that land in the NFL than any other state. That's pretty good when you consider that the state of Florida annually will produce anywhere from 200 to 300 solid college prospects. Mississippi has had a fantastically great year if 30 to 40 high school players are considered top notch. Latest NCAA figures support the fact that Mississippi is a top producer of Division I players. Mississippi, according to 1991 figures, was the fourth best producer in the nation; the state churned out 224 players in Division I out of 10,360 high school football players, for a player- produced-per-thousand figure of 216. Hawaii was first with 96 players out of 3,407 high school performers. Florida was second with an amazing 768 players out of 29,093 prepsters, and Louisiana, surprisingly, was third with 344 Division I players out of 15,640 prep players. California was fifth with 1,545 Division I football players out of 75,184 players. Here is the complete list for comparison:

State	DI-91	HS-91	P/M	State	DI-91	HS-91	P/M
1. Hawaii	96	3,407	282	26. West Virginia	60	6,328	95
2. Florida	768	29,093	264	27. Washington	182	20,350	89
3. Louisiana	344	15,640	220	28. Wyoming	22	2,488	88
4. Mississippi	224	10,360	216	29. Missouri	181	21,290	85
5. California	1,545	75,184	205	30. Navada	38	4,475	85
6. Ohio	876	43,551	201	31. Kansas	123	14,857	84
7. Kentucky	149	8,365	178	32. Oregon	91	11,775	77
8. Pennsylvania	451	25,830	175	33. New York	200	31,698	63
9. New Mexico	86	5,010	172	34. Tennessee	134	23,050	58
10. Georgia	378	22,248	170	35. New Hampshire	12	2,097	57
11. Colorado	196	12,251	169	36. Alaska	7	1,269	55
12. Virginia	276	17,563	157	37. Massachusetts	85	16,055	53
13. Maryland	151	9,772	157	38. Iowa	108	20,423	53
14. N. Carolina	306	19,772	155	39. Connecticut	33	7,189	46
15. Alabama	314	21,532	146	40. Minnesota	76	17,259	44
16. Oklahoma	185	13,768	134	41. Wisconsin	106	24,350	44
17. S. Carolina	186	15,390	134	42. Idaho	32	7,581	42
18. Texas	1,422	125,123	114	43. Rhode Island	5	1,681	30
19. Michigan	474	41,960	113	44. Delaware	6	2,166	28
20. Arizona	140	12,484	112	45. N. Dakota	8	3,128	26
21. Indiana	225	20,739	108	46. Montana	15	5,928	25
22. New Jersey	281	25,984	108	47. Arkansas	82	34,744	23
23. Illinois	468	47,238	99	49. Maine	5	3,013	17
24. Nebraska	119	12,138	98	50. Vermont	2	1,371	15
25. Utah	69	7,180	96	Source: Gannett News Service			

Key to Heading: **DI** (Division I Players produced in 1991)
HS-91 (Total High School football players in 1991)
P/M (Players per thousand playing Division I football)

The coaching of high school players in the state is handled quite capably by young and progressive high school coaches that blend in with the crusty old prep veterans. The Mississippi Association of Coaches is one of the largest coaching organizations in the U.S. With 82 counties in Mississippi and a huge number of high schools that play football, you can see that the vast number of coaches produces solid talent teachers. The summer convention of the MAC is a lavish and massive undertaking. Annually, the MAC brings in outstanding collegiate and professional coaches to speak to the ranks about improving their craft. The association sponsors the Mississippi High School All-Star football, basketball, soccer, softball, and baseball games. The MAC Coaches Hall of Fame is filled with famous high school and junior college coaches, and the annual banquet for this Hall of Fame attracts nearly 1,000 people every year.

Top notch also describes junior college and community college football in Mississippi. There are 16 JUCO football programs in the state of Mississippi. There is heavy competition among the teams that stretch all across the state in remote areas. Mississippi is a red-hot bed of JUCO talent, and the Magnolia State teams are annually contending for the national JUCO title or nationally ranked in some way. In fact, Mississippi produces as many top recruits in the JUCO ranks as Texas and California, two other states that churn them out in mass numbers. Mississippi JUCOs are rated the best players east of the Mississippi, and most of them were originally signed by larger schools in the SEC or elsewhere. The only other JUCOs east of the "Father of Waters" that emphasize football are located in the Carolinas or the New York area. Surrounding states such as Louisiana, Alabama, Tennessee, Georgia and even Florida cannot match the JUCO football programs in Mississippi, if they have those grid programs at all. Small wonder that other schools flood the state in December, January, and February looking for players.

Mississippi is overloaded with college football programs. With 16 JUCO and nine NCAA programs, you have to wonder where all of the players come from. Sometimes, the local sports media is amazed when one of the programs rises up and has a tremendously successful season. They ask:: "How can they do that when the depth on the squad is so thin?" Yet Mississippi collegiate football is rich with championship-caliber talent and pretty solid winning traditions. Mississippi collegiate teams have distinguished themselves in all of the major sports the NCAA has to offer.

So that you can get the characters right, here is a thumbnail look at the "Big Three", the "SWAC Attack," the "Dynamic Duo," and the "Mighty Majors," the gridiron schools of Mississippi.

THE BIG THREE

The "Big Three" are Ole Miss, State, and Southern, as they are commonly called in Mississippi. Ole Miss and State have been members of the Southeastern Conference—the SEC—since the conference was formed in 1933. USM is a relative newcomer on the football scene and is a former member of the old NCAA "small college" division. Today, all of the "Big Three" are members of the NCAA Division IA—the highest classification for an NCAA member that participates in athletics.

The University of Mississippi, known as Ole Miss, is located in the northeast part of the state in Oxford, Mississippi. Under Coach Johnny Vaught from 1947 to 1970, the Rebels won six SEC titles and a national championship in 1960 with the Football Writers Association of America award of the Grantland Rice Trophy. The Rebels set bowl records in the '50s, '60s and early '70s by going to 17 consecutive bowls, but fell on hard times in the early and mid-1980s. Billy Brewer, who played under the legendary Vaught, was hired to take over the Ole Miss football team in 1983, and he is now the second winningest coach in school history behind Vaught. Brewer has guided the Rebels to five bowls in his 10-year tenure. Ole Miss has a solid football tradition, a horrible basketball tradition (only two major tourney titles and one NCAA appearance in 1981 when the Rebs won the SEC Tournament), and a pretty fair baseball history. The Rebel diamond squads, however, have been in a slump for a decade. Ole Miss legend Donnie Kessinger, a baseball and basketball All-American for the Red and Blue and former player and/or manager of the St. Louis Cardinals, Chicago Cubs, and Chicago White Sox leads the diamond Rebs. New Rebel basketball coach Rob Evans is attempting to forge out a foundation for Ole Miss basketball. Lady Rebel basketball under Van Chancellor has a national reputation as being one of only four schools to go to all of the NCAA women's basketball tournaments until the

20

streak was broken in 1993. (Tennessee, Long Beach State, and Louisiana Tech are the others.) The Rebels celebrated 100 Years of Football, A Century of Heroes, in 1993.

Mississippi State is located in east Mississippi in Starkville. The Bulldogs have one only one SEC title, in 1941, and they have had a dreadful football history. State has had success under former coach and athletic director Bob Tyler in the 1970s and limited success under other coaches such as Emory Bellard in the 1980s. Overall, the Dawgs have only been to seven bowls. Currently, State is coached by Jackie Sherrill, who guided MSU to the 1991 Liberty Bowl and the 1992-93 Peach Bowl, their first bowl appearances in 10 years. State does have an impeccable reputation in college baseball under Ron Polk, with numerous SEC titles and trips to NCAA regionals in the last 10 years. Richard Williams and his basketball Bullies won the regular season SEC crown in 1991 and their hoops tradition is on the upswing after a long hiatus from the early '60s under Bailey Howell.

The University of Southern Mississippi is a southern independent school located in the south part of the state in Hattiesburg. The Golden Eagles of USM have had some successes in football in the mid-1980s under former coaches Bobby Collins, Jim Carmody, and Curley Hallman. They have a unique habit of being the underdog who rises to knock off the favorites, since they have the smallest budget in the state to work with. Their current coach is Jeff Bower, who quarterbacked at USM in the 1970s. USM has gone to six bowls, all of the minor variety, but some of their biggest wins include beating an Alabama Bear Bryant squad at his final home game at Tuscaloosa in 1982 by the score of 38-29. USM is forging out basketball tradition under M. K. Turk—they won the 1990 Metro conference regular season and NIT titles, and Hill Denson took the Eagles to their first ever NCAA regional appearance in baseball in 1991. The basketball and baseball teams are affiliated with the Metro Conference. Ole Miss, State and Southern annually compete against teams that have two to three times the enrollments of The Big Three. Most SEC schools have student bodies that range from 20,000 to 30,000 while the combined enrollments of The Big Three barely reaches 30,000.

THE SWAC ATTACK

There are three Division IAA schools located in Mississippi, and they are all members of the SWAC—Southwest Athletic Conference. They are predominantly black colleges, with a strong history of football excellence.

Jackson State is an urban college located in downtown Jackson. The JSU Blue Bengals captured numerous SWAC titles under former coach W. C. Gorden, but they have never advanced past the first round in the NCAA Division IAA playoffs, a jinx that still bothers the squad. Jackson State features numerous alumni that have distinguished themselves in the pro ranks. The most famous graduate has to be Columbia native Walter Payton, the all time running back in the NFL and a Mississippi legend.

Alcorn State is located on the east banks of the Mississippi River south of Vicksburg and Port Gibson at tiny Lorman. Alcorn State is the chief rival of Jackson State and has won several SWAC titles. Alcorn has a tiny budget, but signs the big recruits. They have numerous alumni in the NFL and the Braves are a defensive back factory. Alcorn's top college star is Steve "Air" McNair, a QB who has shattered all school passing rrecords, and was touted as a Heisman Trophy candidate.

Mississippi Valley State is located in the Mississippi Delta at diminutive Itta Bena. The Delta Devils have only had football since the 1950s and they struggle with absolutely the smallest budget in the SWAC and in Mississippi. Where else would you find the athletic director serving as a sports information director as Chuck Prophet has to do? Valley's most famous alumnus is, without a doubt, Jerry Rice of the San Francisco 49ers, one of the greatest wide receivers in the history of the NFL.

THE DYNAMIC DUO

Mississippi features two schools—blood rivals—that are members of Division II of the NCAA football classes. Both schools are members of the Gulf South Conference and have been successful in football, basketball, and baseball from year to year.

Mississippi College is located in Clinton, Mississippi, a suburb of

Jackson to the west. The MC Choctaws won the 1989 Division II National Championship in football and made it to the national semifinals in 1990. MC has produced several NFL stars and competes with the big schools for recruits on an annual basis. MC is a private school that commands big bucks for tuition and receives enormous alumni donations.

Shockingly, Mississippi College was stripped of its 1989 National Title in football when it was hit hard with NCAA probation in January, 1993. In the harshest NCAA penalty ever issued to a Mississippi institution of higher learning, MC received the following sanctions:

—Banned from the 1993 and 1994 NCAA Division II play-offs.
—Ineligible for TV appearances in 1993.
—Banned from off-campus recruiting during the 1993-94 academic year.
—Banned from offering new scholarships to new players in 1993-94.
—Limited to 30 scholarships in 1993-94 and 1994-95.
—No expense-paid recruiting visits during the 1993-94 academic year.
—Stripped of the 1989 NCAA Division II National Football Championship.
—Placed on *four years* probation.

The NCAA landed hard on the Choctaws because they had 80 players on scholarship—double the limited number of 40—from 1989 to 1990. It took MC's administration 13 months to discover that they had double the number of football players on scholarship, which is a $100,000 miscue. The school pointed fingers at ex-coach John Williams, who was fired for matters totally unrelated to the NCAA probe but never completely revealed by the school. The school also supposedly tried to clean up its act. The NCAA, however, reported that the self-imposed restrictions were not followed.

The result? A lost national title and a soiled reputation for a private Baptist college that prides itself on integrity, honesty, and acting in a Christian forthright manner.

Delta State is located in the Mississippi Delta in Cleveland, Mississippi. The Statesmen (or you may use the "politically correct nickname of the "Fightin' Okra") are known more for their women's basketball program and baseball teams than the football team. Basketball Hall of Famer Lucia Harris led the Lady Statesmen to three straight national titles in hoops in the 1970s in the women's classification prior to the creation of the NCAA women's tournament. The Lady Statesmen won three national titles in Division II in the late 1980s and 1990s. The baseball team, formerly coached by Boston Red Sox pitcher Dave "Boo" Ferris, captured conference and national titles on the diamond for years. Delta State has tried to improve its athletic status in football recently by playing Southern Mississippi and Mississippi Valley in Hattiesburg and Jackson, respectively.

THE MIGHTY MAJORS

Millsaps is a private college located in downtown Jackson. The Division III Majors have been a football powerhouse for years. Under former coach Harper Davis, the Majors were legendary for going undefeated every year and mysteriously not getting invited to the Division III playoffs. Known more for its academics and than for its athletics, Millsaps, due to its classification, offers no athletic scholarships, yet they attract top athletes due to their tradition of excellence. The Majors belong to the SCAC conference and won the SCAC title in football in 1991, the first year they competed in the SCAC. Millsaps, however, was still ignored for the Division III playoffs, a continual snub and sore spot for Millsaps alums and fans.

THE JUCOS

Mississippi has become a recruiting haven for junior college/community college football programs. When teams across the south cannot get a player in due to NCAA rules and eligibility requirements, they sometimes "place" a player into a JUCO program that is relatively close. Most of those players, ironically, end up in Mississippi because of the emphasis on football.

The program at Northwest Mississippi Community College located in Senatobia, (just south of Memphis) may be the best JUCO football program in the nation. Led by former Ole Miss quarterback Bobby Franklin, the Northwest Rangers are perennial champions in JUCO football and they frequently face NEO, Northeast Oklahoma, in national title football games. The Rangers captured the 1992 national championship with a powerhouse team.

Other Mississippi JUCO teams that usually feature "placed" players include Itawamba CC at Fulton (near Tupelo), Hinds CC (near Jackson at Raymond), Holmes CC (Goodman), Jones County CC (Ellisville near Laurel) Mississippi Delta (Moorhead), and Gulf Coast CC (just north of Gulfport). The remaining JUCO programs (Coahoma, East Central, Copiah-Lincoln, Meridian, Mary Holmes, Northeast, Pearl River and Southwest) do not feature as many top-notch recruits as the other programs, but they still produce solid recruiting bases for college coaches.

In addition to these football playing schools, there are NAIA schools such as Belhaven in Jackson and William Carey in Hattiesburg that field extremely competitive basketball and baseball teams. These tiny schools occasionally will sign up players that the Big Three want to sign for their programs.

Currently, the university system in Mississippi is in a confused state of change thanks to a recent U.S. Supreme Court decision entitled *Ayers vs. Fordice*, et al. Mergers and closings of Mississippi Valley, Alcorn, and the "W" (Mississippi University for Women at Columbus, which competes in women's sports and joined the Gulf South Conference recently) have been proposed and further litigation regarding the university structure and a desegregation of that system is embroiled in the U.S. District Court according to Supreme Court directives. The *Ayers* case may change the face of college athletics in the Magnolia State, but that subject will surely end up in another book by someone else.

Now that you know a little about the characters, know this: every member of the "Big Three" has been placed on NCAA probation for violations relating to their football programs since the late 1970s. Mississippi State was the first state team to get hit with probation in 1977-78 under former head coach and athletic director Bob Tyler, and it cost Tyler his coaching career.

State's transgression was playing a defensive lineman named Larry Gillard, who was declared ineligible by the NCAA when it was determined that he received free clothing from State alumni who owned a clothing store. MSU was placed on a two-year probation, but painfully, they had to forfeit each and every game in which Gillard stepped out onto the field. The Bulldogs were forced to declare 18 games as forfeits, many of which they had won from the 1975, 1976, and 1977 seasons.

MSU was hit by the NCAA folks in the early stages of the Great Probation Drive by the organization that would hit a peak with penalties in the mid to late 1980s. State even challenged the NCAA in their home county of Oktibbeha where Starkville is located. The school sued the NCAA on behalf of MSU football player Larry Gillard in the Mississippi Chancery Court and attempted to halt the sanctions by a local injunction. State argued that Gillard's constitutional rights had been violated and he had been denied due process by the NCAA hearing methods.

In a 1977 landmark decision entitled *NCAA vs. Gillard,* 352 So.2d 1072 (Miss. 1977), the Mississippi Supreme Court reversed the Oktibbeha County Chancellor's actions and dissolved the court order that halted the NCAA from imposing probation and forfeiture of wins. In a unanimous opinion, Mississippi's highest court declared that Gillard's rights had been protected by the NCAA procedure, and that a football player's "right" to play college football was not a "property right" that fell within the due process clause of the State or Federal Constituion.

State had to serve the probation after losing in court. The NCAA was the winner, as they prove to be so often in court disputes.

Southern Mississippi was next on the probation roll. USM was caught in recruiting improprieties in the early '80s. The infractions were incurred under the reign of Bobby Collins. But Collins left for SMU in Dallas, and the Golden Eagles served their penalty under Jim Carmody. In a twist of irony, Collins would soon be in charge of an SMU Mustang football program that would receive the harshest penalty in the history of the NCAA: the so-called Death Penalty. SMU was hit after 1986 and the football team was ordered to cease operations in 1987. The Mustangs have yet to recover from Bobby Collins' years at the rich Dallas school. Ironically, Collins is now back at USM in charge of fundraising efforts.

Ole Miss is still recovering from the probation placed on them in 1986 as well. The Rebels are the last of the "Big Three" that got hit by the NCAA. Once considered a "pet school" by NCAA enforcers according to former NCAA investigator Brent Clark, the Rebels had the book thrown at them for recruiting violations. Ole Miss was charged with illegally providlng funds for high school student athletes to go to Ole Miss football camps in the summer through the Rebel

Club of Jackson. Further, the Rebels were charged with illegally recruiting Wayne Martin, a defensive lineman from the state of Arkansas who inked with the Razorbacks and now plays in the NFL for the New Orleans Saints.

Ole Miss had to attend the NCAA infractions committee meetings in late 1986, while they headed towards what might be an SEC championship year. The Rebels had just upset LSU in Baton Rouge 21-19 on national TV, and if they could beat Tennessee in home stadium Mississippi Veterans Memorial in Jackson and State the next week, they would be SEC regular season champs for the seventh time.

With hearings scheduled in Kansas on Sunday, however, beating the Vols was the last thing on the minds of Ole Miss officials and coaches. Tennessee won 22-10 in a game in which Ole Miss led going into the fourth quarter. The next day, the Rebels had to be before a committee to decide the fate of the school's athletic future. The Rebs were placed on a two-year probation, but only got one year of sanctions, meaning no bowl or TV appearances for 1987. Ole Miss was also forced to eliminate a very good assistant coach, Mickey Merritt, and they darned near lost Billy Brewer in a power struggle with the new chancellor of the university, Gerald Turner.

With no incentives or solid goals for their season, Ole Miss limped to a 3-8 year in 1987. The year could have been brighter, but in the first game against Memphis State in Memphis, Ole Miss failed to score on 4th down and inches at the Tiger goal line and lost 16-10. The season spiraled downward after that and the 1987 Rebels had quit in spirit and on the field.

As a postscript to the Ole Miss probation, the Rebels rebuilt in 1988 with a 5-6 record and then went bowling in 1989 with a 7-4 slate and a Liberty Bowl win over Air Force, and a sparkling 1990 9-2 record where they went to the Gator Bowl. The Rebels nearly captured the SEC regular season crown against, you guessed it, Tennessee. The Vols won that one in a nationally televised game by CBS, 22-13.

That's the effect the NCAA can have on you if you break the rules these days—forfeits, death penalties, lost championships, lost seasons, lost revenue from TV and bowl money. It's a serious problem if the NCAA comes calling through its infractions committee. Incredibly, the NCAA woes for the "Big Three" pale in comparison to the Mississippi College probation of 1993. By far, the NCAA penalties on the

Choctaw football program are the most serious ever levied on any athletic team of any type in the state. MC is now suffering a form of embarrassment unknown in their school history. MC did not appeal the four-year probation, loss of scholarships, loss of recruiting privileges, and the horrifying loss of a National Division II Championship.

Interestingly enough, Jacksonville State, who lost 3-0 to MC, in the title game, refused to accept the National Championship trophy, explaining that they had not won the title on the field. A lot of very good players suffered because a football coach and staff and a lousy administration had twice as many players on scholarship as allowed under the rules. That whole concept is unthinkably stupid in the days where the NCAA points to institutional control as the be-all and end-all to problems in recruiting. Just consider—a national title down the tubes because somebody can't count heads!

It should be pointed out that in each and every case involving the "Big Three," Mississippi College, and their woes with Mission, Kansas, the probation brought some measure of success to the schools. Eventually, recruits brought in under those infraction times would take the teams to bowls. In the case of MC, a national title was achieved but stripped away due to the violations. That's a sad commentary on the price you would pay to have a winning season and reap in the TV and bowl monies.

Today, all of the "Big Three" Mississippi programs are NCAA clean, but how long can it last with the invading recruiting forces that strike from anywhere in the South? The pressure on these teams to succeed is tremendous, since they carry the financial burden of all of the athletic programs such as baseball, track, and other minor sports. The "Big Three" of Mississippi do not carry the budgets of other rich teams in the SEC and ACC such as Tennessee, LSU, Alabama, Auburn, Georgia, or Florida State. That's a fact of life that the coaches, administrators, staffs, fans and alumni live with every time they follow their team.

Take a look at recent figures published by *USA Today* of the schools' recruiting budgets and how they compare:

28

College	Football recruiting budget	Basketball recruiting budget
Ole Miss	$250,639.	$80,965.
Miss. State	$163,994.	$98,712.
Southern Miss.	$ 60,850.	$29,783.

(Basketball figures combine men's and women's programs.)

Now compare those budgets to the following SEC teams and other schools:

College	Football recruiting budget	Basketball recruiting budget
Alabama	$226,382.	$118,350.
Arkansas	$161,573.	$ 67,985.
Auburn	$190,052.	$ 97,164.
Florida	$354,993.	$167,941.
Georgia	$390,000.	$153,286.
Kentucky	$243,938.	$231,976.
LSU	$ 68,901.	$ 22,482.
South Carolina	$317,488.	$ 47,523 sports
Tennessee	$530,911. (men's sports)	$ 76,448. (women's sports)
Vanderbilt	$317,712. (men's sports)	$ 20,904. (women's sports)

Even more mind-boggling are the revenue and expenditure figures of the top football colleges in the nation. Alabama is number one with $13.2 million earned from the football team, not counting NCAA, TV or SEC monies distribution. Bama spent over $6 million to be first in revenue in the nation. Florida State hauled in nearly $12 million and spent nearly $5.5 million to keep the program running smoothly and in second place among the big gainers and spenders. Miami was third with $18 million being placed in the coffers. Teams such as Notre Dame, Syracusc, Michigan, Georgia, and Tennessee have massive budgets and receive massive infusions of capital each year.

Comparatively, Ole Miss had football revenue in 1992 of $6.4 million and total expenses of $4.6 million. Those expenses covered the whole ball of wax—salaries, scholarships, travel, recruiting, operations, debt service, etc., etc. Bama outspent Ole Miss by $1.4 million in 1992, a wide disparity in college athletics..

As another example of the obstacles Mississippi teams face, in the 1991-1992 recruiting season, Jeff Bower's USM staff was so limited by their budget that none of the assistants traveled by air to visit recruits. The Golden Eagles were limited to the state of Mississippi and the area in a 400-mile radius from Hattiesburg for their recruiting territory. The motto of the recruiting staff was "If you can't drive to see them in a day, you can't recruit them."

Ole Miss, State, and Southern annually compete against teams and universities that can produce big bucks in recruiting wars, and that which makes it all the more tougher when Signing Day rolls around. Despite the budgetary disadvantages, the "Big Three" do shine every now and then. In 1992, for only the fourth time in three decades, all of the "Big Three" had winning records in football in the same year. The only other times this has happened were in the years 1963, 1975, and 1986. Further, 1992 marked the first time in almost 30 years that Ole Miss and Mississippi State received bowl bids in the same season (a win in the Liberty Bowl for Ole Miss over Air Force, and a loss in the Peach for State to North Carolina).

That's amazing considering that recruiting in Mississippi is no bowl of cotton these days!

CHAPTER 4
Signing Day

NO DAY IN American sports is quite like Signing Day for Division I football recruits. It has become a ritual in the South, a literal day of reckoning. Strange things happen on this day to aspirations of fans, coaches, players, and high schoolers everywhere. Every team "filled their needs." Every team "signed their limit." Every team "signed some quality athletes and good citizens." Every team "netted some blue chippers."

One thing's for sure, the pressure is finally popped like a festering blister on Signing Day. The suspense is, for the most part, over, and fans and coaches can settle back into the normal routine of life, whatever that may be. The day itself might be anticlimatic if all of the team's commitments sign as expected.

But Signing Day is also the day of the unexpected and the surprises. The last minute changes of heart and power plays exhibited by recruits and coaches alike are incredible. What's more incredible is the reaction of the fans and media in the South to the news generated by the athletic departments of all of the southern colleges. It's a given that the local radio call-in shows are completely jammed with information about Signing Day. Live remotes for both TV and radio crews are quite common with Signing Day ceremonies being performed at high schools and player homes across the South.

The media may not enjoy this day because of the phone calls and pressure from their listeners, viewers, and readers to put the information out, but that's the demand that recruiting followers have created. The media hates it all simply because of all the rumors, hearsay, and untruths that pop up—stuff they just can't pin down in print or on the air. Just as important as the coverage is the commentary, as most fans want to hear just how the recruiting classes rate among other schools and programs. This is when the recruiting gurus come out of hiding and place their faces to their voices with constant interviews about who signed whom and why.

In Mississippi, there is nothing quite like Signing Day. It is a day that is coveted almost as much as the first game of the football season in the fall. I often wish I had a percentage of each and every phone call, 900 or otherwise, that was placed in the state on "S-Day." I believe I could safely say that I could retire on that percentage and wouldn't have to write this book!

Following Mississippi recruiting wouldn't be complete unless you made the rounds on Signing Day. Many fans flock to the athletic department offices or the football offices to view large chalkboards where staff members write in names of signees as they are confirmed. In days past, these events were like huge pep rallies and the crowds would even gasp at the new names being chalked up. Fans and followers would stand around, in a hopeful frame of mind, with lists in hand and they would mentally "pencil in" recruits into their lineups. Naturally, all of the signees could start in the fall and contribute immediately. Hint. Hint. Wink. Wink.

Much of that has died down with the NCAA "Fax and FedEx" rule where players may not be confirmed as being signed until one or two days after Signing Day. Ole Miss, for the first time in decades, declined to put up the big chalkboard in the athletic offices because of the rule and the crowds died down for 1992. The blackboard reappeared in 1993 and a record turnout swamped the athletic offices. If a basketball game is played that night on campus, however, the crowds still show up in large numbers. If a "super" class is anticipated by the fans, the athletic departments brace their offices for an explosion of people. Head coaches and their assistants take on a "bunker" mentality during the day and they emerge in the afternoon or late evening after word comes in from many of their recruits. You wouldn't want to be too visible if you're a football coach on signing day ,since alumni and fans would mob you for the latest poop.

Local radio and TV stations also arrive early and stay late during signing day at the athletic offices. Play-by-play announcers such as David Kellum of Ole Miss, John Cox of Southern Mississippi and, Jim Ellis of Mississippi State virtually camp out at the athletic department offices with their "Marti" mobile units and other equipment for remote broadcasts. As the S.I.D. staff doles out the latest names, the announcers interrupt their regular radio programming as if it was all some kind of war update. Edward R. Murrow would surely be rolling over in his grave if he ever heard one of these broadcasts. That's quite an evolution from the London rooftops in World War II to college campuses!

TV guys usually film or do some live shots in the evening. Mostly, the TV guys are shooting the signings live at local high schools where Signing Day ceremonies are akin to world leaders signing summit day accords. Recruits contact the media to let them know where and when they will "declare" their future school loyalty. As the TV crews gather at school libraries and gyms, these players concoct a grandiose entrance of some sort to announce where they will sign. If they don't sign at school, the camera crews speed toward the hot recruit's home, where a circus of immense proportions happens.

The really strange practice that has emerged in Mississippi is the advent of "Recruiting Parties" or "Signing Day Slings." Recruiting parties were created in Jackson, Mississippi, exclusively to fulfill the insatiable needs of recruiting junkies and rabid alumni and fans. Since the mid 1980s, followers of Ole Miss, Mississippi State, Southern Mississippi and LSU have gathered somewhere in Jackson on Signing Day to compare notes and recruits. These parties are not your usual social mixers and no other state in the U.S. has anything to compare as far as anyone knows.

The largest and one of the oldest of these parties has to be the blast put on by the Rebel Club of Jackson. This party is held annually at Jimmie Lyles Carpets just across the Pearl River in Flowood, Mississippi, down busy Lakeland Drive. T. J. Anderson is the owner of Lyles Carpets and, since 1983, he has loaned out his facility and his carpet warehouse in the back to allow Rebel Clubbers to come in and gaze at cardboard posters listing signees not just of Ole Miss, but of all of the local colleges and top rivals. T. J. became involved in this madhouse affair when then-Rebel Club president Jon Turner, an accountant and a good one by trade, told T. J. how he wanted to do something different with the club on Signing Day.

"Jon and I were talking one day and he mentioned that he really would like to do something different on Signing Day and he said we really need a big place," said T. J. "I said, 'Hey, I've got a big warehouse, why don't we do it in there,' and that's how it started."

ANNUAL
★ ★ **RECRUITING PARTY** ★ ★

Date: **WEDNESDAY, FEBRUARY 3, 1993**

Time: **5:30 p.m. Drinks and Bar-B-Q**

Location: **Jimmie Lyles Carpet**
Lakeland Drive

★ ★ ★

Full Year Paid Members - No Charge
Regular Members - $8.00
Non-Members - $12.00

Guests Welcome

An average crowd of over 200 loyal Rebels crams into T. J.'s carpet warehouse on Signing Day where they dine on former Rebel running back Doug Cunningham's barbeque (he owns a Gridley's restaurant in Jackson) and toss it back with several adult beverages. Yes, you can catch the phrase "*Heard Anything?*" by anybody new who walks in. The party starts at about four in the afternoon and rolls until everybody gives out talking about 25 signees listed on that cardboard poster. Keep in mind that you will meet all sorts of professional people in the warehouse—guys and a few gals that have well-paying jobs, families, futures, and plenty of other things to do besides reading poster boards in a carpet warehouse.

In T. J.'s words: "It seems to get a little bigger and a little better every year. It's a lot of fun and I think there are people that never come to the regular Rebel Club meetings, but they come to this meeting because of the excitement and the anticipation."

Does that sound like your typical party among sports fans? Again, these are doctors, lawyers, bankers, dentists, laborers, accountants, insurance agents, people of all walks of life. Anticipation and excitement over a poster board with names? Are you kidding me? T. J. has to punt business on Signing Day. Because they think he has some link to recruiting inside information, Ole Miss fans, and fans of other schools for that matter, will call Lyles Carpets constantly throughout the day for the latest. Lists are not posted in the warehouse until 4:30 P.M., but that doesn't faze your average lunatic fringe recruiting nut. Talk about calling the folks on the carpet!

T. J.'s employees, of course, have no idea or concept about what is going on, so T. J. has to answer nearly every call. After all, T. J.'s workers are used to selling carpet, not following the progress of 18 and 19 year old football players and where they will attend college. T. J. explains: "One of the really unique things for me is that during the day we get phone calls from all over the country as if we really knew what was going on! We usually can't answer their questions, but we've had people call from Washington, D.C. to Seattle, Washington, during the day asking questions. I'm just waiting for an overseas call."

For the record, 1991 saw a call come in from an Ole Miss fan in North Dakota, and they fielded a call from Rebels in Alaska in

1992. T. J. has received calls from Rebels working on off-shore oil rigs in the Gulf of Mexico south of New Orleans. Add to all those calls the frequent callers from Louisiana, Alabama, Georgia, Tennessee, Arkansas, and all points on the map in the state of Mississippi and you have quite a collection and a nicely overloaded phone circuit. The calls still amaze T. J. to this day. The *number* of the calls amazes me.

This particular recruiting party is even responsible for the installation of a traffic light. In 1985, the overflow around Lakeland Drive was so heavy from the recruiting party, T. J. had to call in the Flowood, Mississippi, police department to direct traffic. Over 400 people, a Signing Day record, crammed in the warehouse that day to sit on huge rolls of carpet and look at those lists and eat that barbeque and consume that highball. Flowood city fathers put in a light to help the flow, which I'm sure thrilled commuters to Jackson. Whoever draws the traffic assignment for the party from Flowood P.D. gets a free plate of barbeque, delivered personally out of gratitude by T. J.

The party has even been good for business and has attracted onlookers who would eventually sample T. J.'s carpet wares. "In the past, they have parked all over the highway. After the party and while we are cleaning up down here, we'll get phone calls from people wanting to know if we are having some kind of a big sale. One year, a lady who noticed the throngs of Red and Blue fans thought T. J. was having a Going Out of Business Sale and it sparked her into getting back into the carpeting business!"

There is nothing quite like this anywhere in the U.S. It's a party that is mentioned across the South on Signing Day. Bill King and Bob Bell of Nashville's WLAC radio (1510 AM a 50,000-watt station that is a hotbed of southern recruiting) mention it every year. As Bob Bell likes to say: "Well, I guess those guys in Jackson are sitting up on those carpet rolls about this time!"

Does T. J. ever get tired of this incredible gathering? He answers: "We hope to do it for another 100 years, at least. We really enjoy it. This party has a lot of carryover. Sometimes, when we sell a roll of carpet in July or August, we'll find a Rebel Club name tag stuck to it left over from this party."

36

Oddly enough, when they find those tags, that's when the guys on the poster board in the back of the warehouse show up on campus to play football!

T. J.'s bash is not the only traditional party in Mississippi on Signing Day. Just a few miles east down the road off Lakeland Drive in Brandon, Mississippi, the Mississippi State Bulldog Club faithful meet to discuss Bully recruits. The site is Cindy's Fish House, owned by a Mississippi State Bulldog Club member named Wayne Hinton, and this gathering has taken place every Signing Day since 1981. At Cindy's, prominent State alumni and supporters meet in the back room with a telephone hookup to speak to the athletic department in Starkville. Like the guys at Lyles Carpets, the State folks have the poster boards and alcohol, but they have good-tastin' down home southern fried catfish for their meal. The Bulldog party is a fine example of what goes on at most of these parties. Most participants gather for a meal after work while checking out signee lists for their school. It's a great chance (or excuse!) for folks to talk sports.

At another part of town and at the same time, the LSU and Southern Miss. crowds gather. The LSU Tigers Unlimited Club meets under the direction of super Tiger Bill Hulsey. The USM faithful meet as the Eagle Club. Both sets of fans use the phone hookups, big meals, poster boards, and whatever else to satisfy their Signing Day curiosity. The Eagle Club crew also meets once a month until football season, and then they meet at noon every Friday, usually at the downtown Jackson Landmark Center. Their numbers may be smaller, but the intensity is just the same. It's all really very crazy!

And the parties are not limited to Jackson. Down on the Gulf Coast in Pascagoula, Mississippi, a bar named Thunder's Tavern hosts a recruiting party each year. Thunder's Tavern is owned by former Ole Miss lineman Thunder Thornton, who played for coach Ken Cooper in the mid-1970s. Thunder is an immensely loyal Ole Miss man and he opens up the bar to Ole Miss fans and fans of other schools on Signing Day. The party, I am told, never stops. It may slow down, but only after all of the signees for the day have been announced.

There are similar parties all across the South on Signing Day.

They may be smaller and more scaled down than the Jackson or Gulf Coast parties, but they all have one thing in common and use the same language: *Heard Anything?*

*****

Signing Day in Mississippi is not limited to the recruiting parties and the silliness that goes on at those affairs during the day. Many other signing nuts will spend hours on the phone, talking to their fellow alumni buddies about what is happening. They call radio call-in shows in the evening in large droves and they flood the 900 lines. There have been plenty of stories of phone line breakdowns where the phone company is overloaded with long distance calls. These out-of-state callers are relocated alumni wanting to know if anybody's "heard anything."

Being a radio sports call-in show host on Signing Day is a lot like being a referee in a fight-filled National Hockey League game! Just when you break up one brawl, another starts up and you have to keep putting out the fires. Before you step in front of that microphone, you better have thoses lists ready and be very up to date on your information. If you don't, you'll get totally buried. There's always some member of the recruiting lunatic fringe ready for the host with some miniscule piece of factoid that will supposedly blow you away on the air.

If the host is smart, he or she will bring on a reporter from the paper who covers recruiting on a regular basis or enlist the services of one of the recruiting gurus. This will cool off the phone lines and put all of the emphasis on the guests. Believe me, those people will hang on every word.

Sometimes, in fact, you wish some of these guys would *actually* hang on every word or a nice short rope. Some callers get worked up in a madness about their signee class and call in to lord it over the other schools. If Ole Miss or State signs a blue chipper, all-stater, and all-around recruit, their fans will call and brag how their class is so much better than Southern's or any other schools. The same goes for USM and so on and so forth.

Keep in mind that many of these players will never be the giant impact players they are projected to be coming out of high school.

Also, there is no way to judge any recruiting class of any university until that class enters its senior year. There is no way to tell if a guy is going to blossom into the next All-Conference All-American that will be drafted by the pros. Those types of players are, in reality, few and very far between. Less than 10 percent of all college players have a legitimate shot at the pros. The rest better get their degrees and prepare for the real world!

Knowing all of this doesn't slow down anyone on the phone on Signing Day. Usually, on Signing Day, my SportsLine show has originated from the studios. On other occasions, I have broadcast the call-in show at recruiting parties, on campus, at bars, and other sites. On this particular day, we decided to stay close to the wire services, make lists and bring in Woody Woodrick of the *Clarion Ledger*. Woody covered the high school beat for the *Clarion* and, after answering the phones and getting ready for the recruiting edition of the *Clarion*, he had agreed to appear with me for a special two-hour edition. Woody was very "up" on recruiting. He had taken a lot of time and used a lot of effort to cover all of the "Big Three" and the smaller schools in recruiting. When you are having to cover nine universities that play NCAA football in the state, then you better know what you're doing and be totally prepared with all of your lists and player biographies.

Our program had progressed on a nice even pace. All of the names of most of the schools had been read off in the first hour and we were taking calls mostly in the second hour. We had already over-analyzed the "Big Three" and we were working on the SWAC schools, MC, Delta State, and Millsaps. We had called all of the recruiting parties we knew of and put them on the air live. Woody and I were both tired since we had been up at the crack of dawn to get the early signees and neither of us had stopped for a breather.

A disgruntled-for-no-apparent-reason USM Golden Eagle fan called in and the conversation went like this:

Glen: Let's go back to the telephones, Woody, SportsLine, you're on the air.....

Caller: Yes, uh, I have to agree with your first caller tonight. I think this show sounds like an Ole Miss fan's show. You really give Southern recruits the short end of the stick! (The hackles on both our necks start to rise!)

Glen: What do you want me to say about Southern's recruits?

Caller: Well, I think it's your job to know something to say about 'em and you obviously don't know what to say!

Glen: Well, tell me about 'em, obviously you know more about them....

Caller: I think you and Woody are an embarrassment to your profession! (That tore it! I looked over at Woody and his face was fire engine red as he exploded over the microphone!)

Woody: You're an idiot! Aw right....Listen, listen, listen! I'm not going to be insulted professionally...

Caller: I'll hang up and listen to your reply.... (Caller hangs up.)

Woody: Listen to this now...

Glen: He hung up.

Woody: Yeah, he's an idiot! See, he'll say his thing and doesn't have to say his name and then he runs and hides! I spend months researching recruiting!....Months researching recruiting!....I've already started on next year's! If these names don't come up it's not my fault! I talk to recruiters, high school coaches....I talk to everybody I can think of that can give me information! And if I don't have the information on the guys, it's not my fault!

Woody didn't calm down for the rest of the show. It's one thing to attack an opinion or rating on a recruiting show. It's quite another thing when you attack the hosts and their reputations. Woody had every right to be offended and upset. He had done a tremendous job of compiling every scrap of profiling information he could. One joker on a call-in show ruined his day and, possibly, his year.

Please keep in mind that fans of *all* schools react in much the same way as this USM caller. Many fans become so intently involved in recruiting wars that their loyalties cloud what their mouths produce.

Again, it illustrates that even when you give these guys all the information you can possibly give, they still want more and more and more and more! By the way, Woody Woodrick no longer works in the *Clarion* Sports Department and does not actively follow recruiting. What does that tell you about this profession as it relates to Signing Day?

40

*****

Not as much excitement is generated when basketball players are signed out of Mississippi. After all, most of them head out of state such as Gulfport's Chris Jackson, who attended LSU, Litterial Green of Moss Point, who became a Georgia Bulldog, Kenny Payne of Laurel, who landed at Louisville, Jackson's James Robinson, Meridian's Derrick McKey, who went to Alabama, and many others. Some stay inside the state, but it is a rare occurrence when one of the "Big Three" can convince an outstanding high school hoopster to go to school close to home.

In terms of basketball signings becoming headline news, 1992 was the greatest year in history for Mississippi signees. The state produced more talent in basketball than any other year probably in the history of recruiting. Two names really stood out in Mississippi: Vandale Thomas of Monticello in Lawrence County, Mississippi, in the southern part of the state, and Othella Harrington from Murrah High in Jackson.

Thomas led his team to the State 4A championship. He was recruited by nearly everybody in the nation and he even met head on with Harrington in a special exhibition game which Lawrence County won against 5A Murrah on state wide pay-per-view TV. In fact, that game pitting the 4A champs against the VA champs was a history making game in terms of telecasting high school basketball—it had never been done before! Basketball recruiting guru Bob Gibbons of Lenoir, North Carolina, even made the trip for this historic occasion and he later said that this event was one of the most exciting hoops happenings he has ever attended—a bold statement for someone who grew up around North Carolina Tarheel basketball. When both players played in the second annual game pitting the best of Mississippi high school players against the best of the Alabama prepsters, fans packed the A. E. Wood Coliseum on the Mississippi College campus in Clinton to the point that people were standing in the aisles and making the local fire marshal very nervous. Scalpers, of all things, were selling $5. tickets for $10. to $25.—for an all star game!

Both players were the subject of constant rumors and both

players waited until after the fall *and* spring signing days had gone by before signing that precious letter of intent. Both players had been spotted making every move imaginable towards whatever school was on the rumor list. Both players kept their preferences shrouded in mystery which was driving nearly everyone who followed recruiting totally bonkers.

If you want to send recruiting gurus and the lunatic fringe into nervous breakdowns, just wait until *after* signing day to ink the letter-of-intent and be sure that no one in the world has any clue as to what you will do or which way you are leaning. That will insure some of these nuts will head for the Valium bottles! No news is surely bad news for these guys.

Thomas had his list down to LSU, Arkansas, and Mississippi State. No other word of commitments or leanings or whatever was coming out of Monticello. A press conference to announce the signing was called at the high school. This is no slap to either Vandale or Othella, but isn't it ironic that most of these signing conferences are held in the school library, a place where many of these recruits across the nation have never been and had to get directions to find it!

After months, days, and hours of speculation, Vandale got ready for his big moment. For many recruits, this is the highlight of their careers. Signing a letter-of-intent by a small town high school hero is nothing short of town celebration. The media was primed and ready with cameras, recorders, and laptop computers. Who would obtain the services of Vandale Thomas?

Five minutes before Thomas walked into the room, he called a very anxious Richard Williams of Miss. State. After all, Williams was hoping to ink one of the top players in the nation, an all-stater, a guy that could step right in and help the Bulldogs. On the phone, Vandale said "Sorry, Coach, but I'm signing with LSU." After Williams' heart dropped, Thomas then said, "Just kidding! Watch the news, coach!" What would most of you give to have a copy of Richard's heart monitor EKG line at that time!

Thomas then entered the room. Trouble is, he was dressed oddly for the occasion. Media members began to snicker and guffaw. Vandale, you see, was wearing Arkansas Razorback gym shorts, a see-through mesh Miss. State Bulldog basketball shirt and he was topped out with a LSU Tiger baseball cap!

Vandale, in a deliberate piece of crassy showmanship, glanced down at the Arkansas pants, the State shirt and doffed the LSU cap while gazing at the Tiger logo.

He then announced he would sign with Miss. State.

Nice stunt, Vandale. When Ringling Brothers rolls through town, we'll dress you with the rest of the clowns!

Then there was Othella.

Harrington proclaimed that he would sign on Monday, May 4, 1992, at the Murrah High Library (there we go talking books again!) at...appropriately....high noon.

You have to understand that this was a player who was academically eligible and that's a high commodity on the recruiting market. He had led his team to two straight 5A titles under his coach, the legendary Orsmond Jordan. He was a scoring, rebounding, dribbling, and blocking machine at 6'-10". He had been highly touted since his *sophomore* year. Coaches had been eyeballing him at Murrah games for over two years. Every college in America, well...almost every college, had tried to sign him.

Rumor upon rumor upon rumor popped up about Othella, but, like Thomas, he kept his cards close to vest. Kentucky fans thought they had him nailed even though he had not taken an official visit to Lexington. North Carolina fans called WLAC in Nashville daily for updates. He was the number one college basketball recruit in America and he knew it. Dick Vitale of ESPN raved about him and so did Billy Packer of CBS. He was on every All-State team, every All-American team, and he had played in all of the top all-star games offered in the country and excelled in all of them. Most all of them had Othella slated to be an NBA lottery pick when he became a collegiate junior.

After he finally signed, CNN Sports had him listed as an NBA draft pick in the high numbers. That's how Harrington's reputation had spread. This was no average recruit.

Harrington kept recruiting buffs baffled for nearly two years. The waiting destroyed several people who followed the teams in line for his possible John Hancock. It got to be old at times, since every reporter would ask him at every opportunity where he was going. Give the kid credit, he never wavered for a second.

His official visits were at Georgetown, Oklahoma, LSU, Miss. State, and Arkansas. His visit with Nolan Richardson at Arkansas went poorly, the rumors claimed. His trip to Oklahoma was a surprise. His trip to State was routine and his trip to Georgetown was pleasant but a long way from home.

LSU appeared to be out because of head coach Dale Brown. This was at the highlight of Dale's adventures with Shaquille O'Neal, the Tiger center who turned pro early and was picked by the Orlando Magic of the NBA. "Daddy Dale" had only recently been involved in a fight on the court with Tennessee forward Carlos Groves after Groves knocked down Shaq on a hard foul during the 1992 SEC basketball tournament in Birmingham. John Thompson of the Hoyas had been to Mississippi to see "O" play on many occasions. Richard Williams of State had openly lobbied for Othella to sign with State on TV interviews. While he failed to mention his name, which would be a NCAA rules violation, he made it clear he wanted the big man. Early bets were on Miss. State with Georgetown and Arkansas running right behind.

May 4, 1992, brought a carnival-like atmosphere to Murrah High School in Jackson. Nearly every media outlet in the area was represented in some capacity and the library was filled to capacity. There were many more fans who could not get in. Most of this crowd had loyalties with the Bulldogs and they could not wait to hear that they had signed one of the top two players in the state and possibly the nation.

It didn't happen for Richard, this time, however. Othella, in a classier display than Vandale Thomas had put on, picked Georgetown. Harrington, with his mom at his side, did have a Hoyas T-shirt for viewing. He said he picked the out-of-state site because John Thompson had experience with big men such as Patrick Ewing and Alonzo Mourning and could prepare him for the pros. He also said it was a lifetime dream for him to go to the Washington, D.C. area college. So much for in-state loyalty.

As the announcement swept through the halls of dear ol' Murrah High, the Bulldog fans that had gathered out front received the bad news as if the president of the U.S. had been shot or their loved ones had been in a serious accident. The long faces and sad expressions told it all. Talk about greed, these fans and alumni had just cruised to maybe the best recruiting class in the history of the school and they wanted it all.

Just think, now, grown men who are influential businesspersons and blue collar workers had just used up their lunch hours to hear where a 6'-10" talented high school basketball player would be going to school for the next two years at least.

If that doesn't make you wonder about the impact of signing day, nothing in this book will!

The TV news broadcasts made Othella's signing with George-town their *lead story*! The *Clarion Ledger* made his signing with the Hoyas *front page news with a huge headline and picture at the top*! In fact, months after "O" had inked with the Hoyas, the *Clarion* was still receiving very heated letters, mostly from disap-pointed State fans, about the coverage that Harrington was garner-ing from a shrinking sports section. As mentioned earlier, the home folks do hold grudges against players going out of state, especially when the have blaring headlines on the front page of the state's largest daily newspaper.

Think about that for a second. With all of the major news stories of the day, are you telling me that the signing of a letter-of-intent by a basketball player dwarfed all of the other serious news of the day? If you answer yes, then we know what fringe you live on and it can't be healthy!

The only incident I can think of in recent memory to match this is the signing of running back Darrell "Lectron" Williams a few years ago. "Lectron" was the most highly sought-after running back out of Prichard, Alabama, in the Mobile area when he was being recruited out of Vigor High. Auburn's Pat Dye was the winner of this recruiting sweepstakes. Darrell committtted to the Tigers in mid-January.

When "Lectron" announced that he would be heading to Auburn in mid-week in mid-afternoon, the Alabama media went bananas. In fact, Mobile TV stations put up a "scroll" on the bottom of their screens announcing that "Lectron" would become a Tiger. That scroll appeared while the afternoon soap operas were being aired! Can you just imagine what your typical Alabama housewife thought about this urgent bulletin in the middle of her daily soap proclaiming that some high school running back was going to Auburn?

Oh, yes, "Lectron" suffered a knee injury that kept him from being a superstar at Auburn. He is no longer on the squad and is out of football. They do say that all fame is fleeting!

*****

Things are not changing about recruits holding on to their choices and decisions. The Harrington and Thomas "teasings" are becoming a very disturbing trend that annoys recruiting followers. Harrington's teammate, Ronnie Henderson, was considered to be one of the top guard prospects in the country in 1992. Henderson, recruited by everybody who's anybody in college basketball, announced in the *Clarion Ledger* that he would not sign or make his decision until the spring signing period in 1993.

Nearly two weeks later, Henderson announced in the same paper that he would sign with LSU in the early signing period in November, 1992. Figure that one out while pondering the recruiting of Eric Dotson, a Pascagoula defensive lineman considered by most to be the top Mississippi football recruit for 1993-93. Eric had his phone disconnected to avoid calls as he has been pursued by all 107 Division IA teams and many other schools across the country. Eric had to stay away from home to avoid the recruiting calls and said that he actually enjoys keeping everyone curious about his choices and preferences. Recruiting gurus complained loudly and openly that they couldn't reach Eric.

The thud you hear in the background is the sound of alumni and fans with heart flutters hitting the floor literally dying to find out where Eric may be attending classes in fall, 1993. Eric signed with Miss. State, after committing to Ole Miss.

*****

On the Morning After the big Harrington circus signing, I entered my neighborhood convenience store to gas up for another daily trip to the Hinds County Courthouse. The owner of the store was attending the register as usual and was checking me out with

46

my gas purchase and my Chocolate Soldier drink. I was a little on the down side.

After all, as an Ole Miss fan, I was hoping my alma mater would go after Othella, but the Rebel coaching staff led by newly fired Ed Murphy apparently didn't make the required effort. As I prepared to leave and cry in my Chocolate Soldier, I noticed another gentleman glancing at the massive *Clarion* headline blasting the fact that Harrington picked Georgetown. This thin man with bronze hair and a sharp mustache stared intently at the lead story, obviously reading it before buying.

He then turned towards the owner at the register and, in a dead serious and unknowing voice, said "Where's Georgetown?"

A huge grin came across my face as I grabbed my drink and headed out. I chimed in: "It's a college in the Washington, D.C. area."

Still serious as a heart attack, the man replied "Oh, I had never heard of it!" and he went about his business. I laughed so hard I split my pants and had to go back home and change clothes.

Refreshing to know sometimes that some people couldn't give a flying flip about recruiting!

Like I mentioned at the start of this chapter, there is no other day in U.S. sports lore quite like Signing Day!

CHAPTER 5
The Dark Side

SIGNING DAY IS a day of great accomplishment and a day of recognition for thousands of high school athletes all over America. For some players, a college scholarship promise means the fulfillment of a lifetime dream and a way out of an economically depressed situation. Prep basketball stars are often signed right out of the urban blighted areas of the U.S. and their signing may represent their way out and a shot at changing their lives.

For all this hopefulness and bright outlook for the college signee, there is a terrible Dark Side to recruiting. If you took a poll of college football and basketball fans, I would be willing to wager that a large majority of those fans would say that college recruiting is infested with cheating and that players are paid in some way to sign with many, if not all, colleges and universities.

How are some of these players paid or obtained by the unscrupulous recruiters? Cars. Houses. Land. Jobs. Salaries. Cash payments in brown bags. Girls. Guys. Drugs. Steroids. Steaks. Hidden tape recorders. Transcripts changed. False letters and information put out by rival schools. Kidnapping. Coercion on the parents. You name it, and somebody has probably provided it or gotten away with it to entice the "innocent prepster" to sign on the dotted line. Much of it sounds like the plot line to a James Bond novel or film. It can be espionage at its finest at times.

You have to understand that if you have bad recruiting classes, you don't win as many football and basketball games. If you don't win many games, you don't go to bowls and tournaments and your games won't be televised. Without TV, bowl or tournament money, your athletic department can become bankrupt if your school is in big time college sports. It's a ripple effect that puts too much emphasis on winning and far too much emphasis on recruiting.

Everybody says every school cheats, so what's the point?

The point is that the NCAA, the National Collegiate Athletic Association, has anointed itself to police this mess. But do they?

The NCAA is a voluntary organization made up of most of the colleges and universities that participate in athletics in some form or fashion. Read that last sentence again—it's a *voluntary* organization where the member schools make the rules through the school presidents, CEOs, chancellors, and athletic directors. If a school is not a member of the NCAA, then they are probably members of the NAIA, the smaller counterpart to the guys in Mission, Kansas.

Speaking of Mission, Kansas, it is ironic that that town is the host city to the main headquarters of the NCAA. It appears these days that the NCAA has forgotten its "mission" when it comes to college athletics.

The NCAA was formed in the late 1800s when college football was coming under immense scrutiny. Too rough and too dangerous was the sport, cried the critics. And too many young men were dying on the fields of play. With no pads, helmets, or very little protection, college football at the turn of the century was one of the roughest sports in the world this side of ice hockey. It was downright deadly.

President Theodore Roosevelt, in fact, pronounced that if college football didn't clean up its act, then he would consider a nationwide ban on the sport. On October 9, 1905, Roosevelt called to the White House a diversified group of football leaders and put it plain on the carpet—make the sport safe or watch it be dismantled across the country. Even though the early meetings after Roosevelt's threatened ban didn't bring up the topic, for its own good and survival, the NCAA emerged as the leader in on-the-field safety. This small band of schools outlined rules and improved the game for the safety of the players, thus saving the sport. If the old "Roughrider" could see the building in Mission and the actions of the past decade, he would surely shake his head in wonder at the transformation of the NCAA from the nation's "Sports Safety Vanguard" to "Policeman of Coaches, Fans, Alumni and Programs."

The 75th convention of the NCAA was held in 1981 and it marked most of the landmark legislation that now controls college athletics. In 1980, the 1980-81 *NCAA Manual* and rule book contained 298 pages and was printed in a softbound volume. Nearly half of that 1980-81 manual involved case rulings on the various rules were contained in the book. The 1991-92 *NCAA Manual* is 479 pages long in a large print book bound with a ring binder. The '91-92 edition has been made "easier to read and comprehend." Most of the rules in these manuals address the subject of collegiate recruitng.

Assistant football coaches must read this book and take a test on it in order to recruit off campus. If they fail, they cannot be certified as off-campus recruiters and they cannot evaluate or go into the field to check on potential high school signees. Head coaches in both football and basketball are extremely limited as to what they can do. The rules limit personal contact, phone calls, types of correspondence that can be sent out and the do's and don'ts of on campus visits. The NCAA has invaded every aspect of recruiting that you can envision.

For example, it was formerly against the rules for a coach to go to see his own son or daughter play high school athletics. It was against the rules for members of teams to go to a teammate's tragic funeral at the expense of the university. It is against the NCAA rules and regulations to print media guides of athletic teams in multi-color or glitzy publications. Now, the media guides are mailed out to recruits and sold to the public under very limited conditions (no newsstand sales) and can only have color pictures on the inside and outside of the back and front covers. The rest of the print in the guide must be the same color!

The NCAA governs what players can enter in terms of contests, drawings, lotteries, or other types of typical everyday recreation. The NCAA even prescribes how and when a player's photo can be used, even if a charity is involved. Indiana basketball player Steve Alford once ran afoul of the rules when he posed (fully clothed) for a sorority calendar for charity. The NCAA altered some of these rules as a result of Alford's involvement and the new changes are now call "the Alford rule."

It is against the rules for a "representative of a university's athletic interests" to even associate with a student athlete ready to sign a college scholarship. This means that if you just so happen to be a season ticket holder to a college athletic team's games, you could conceivably be considered a "representative of the university's athletic interests." The NCAA calls this person a "booster." A totally inno- cent average person could, theoretically, place an entire multimillion dollar collegiate athletic program in jeopardy. What nonsense!

The rule that has probably changed the face of recruiting more than any other rule has to be the "30-95" Rule. When it was created in the early 1980s it meant the end of an era and the end of college football and basketball teams stockpiling players. The "30-95" Rule simply means this: a college football team can award 30 new football scholarships each year, but they could have no more than 95 players on scholarship on the squad. The rule has been lessened recently to 25 new scholarships to give and 85 players total on the team on scholarship. The 25 new scholarship rule has been in effect for several years, while the new 85 limit starts in the mid-1990s.

In the old days, teams could sign as many players when they wanted however they wanted. Alabama, under Paul "Bear" Bryant, was famous for having as many as 200 players on campus at one time. Out of 200 at a time, it was no wonder he found all the best players! In the SEC, there were even *two* Signing Days. There was a December Signing Day when recruits could sign an SEC letter-of-intent. That letter-of-intent bound that player to that SEC school and this method prevented conference teams from raiding each other for players. The player would still have to sign a national letter-of-intent on the regular Signing Day. That practice was eliminated by the NCAA and so was stockpiling.

And in case you may be confused, players sign a document on Signing Day referred to as the letter-of-intent. This letter-of-intent must be signed by the player and his or her parents or guardians. The letter-of-intent binds that player to that school and that school to that player. In other words, if the player meets the minimum eligibility requirements of that particular college, then the school must offer that player an athletic scholarship. The scholarship papers that bind the school financially are actually signed in August just before classes start or initially filled out on Signing Day. In that way, the requirements are shored up, if necessary, and the player and coach solidify their agreement to come to that school.

For any player to be academically eligible for NCAA standards, that player must have a least a 2.00 grade point average in high school courses known as the "core curriculum." The core curriculum includes math, science, social studies, English, and other specified equivalent courses. Along with this 2.00 GPA, the player must also make at least a 17 on the ACT or a 700 on the SAT. The NCAA has produced a sliding scale that combines GPA with ACT or SAT scores. A player who has a 2.00 GPA *only*, must make an ACT score of 21 or an SAT score of 900. This scale has come under criticism from minority groups as they claim this is unfair due to the nature of the standardized testing of the SAT and ACT services.

A player that is a potential college recruit usually receives material explaining all of these requirements. In addition, college coaches are required to provide that information plus graduation rates. The NCAA publishes a guide for the student athlete, and some conferences, such as the SEC, also publish a guide for the prospect. Even though the academic requirements are spelled out to the player in complete detail, some recruits fail to take the ACT or SAT until the last possible moment. When that player fails to make the required score, he loses a scholarship and that university loses a player.

The player must then be considered what is called a "Prop 48" player. A Prop 48 is a player that may have qualified in one part on the academics and failed to qualify on the other. He or she may have the ACT/SAT score, but not the GPA. If that's the case, the player is totally ineligible and must go the JUCO route. The most common scenario is for the player to have the core GPA, but come up short on the ACT/SAT score. If that occurs, the player may enter school under strict limitations, but they cannot participate in athletics for one full school year and their grades must be on a course towards graduation. They also lose a year of eligibility. SEC teams are strictly limited as to how many Prop 48s they can sign and that number is nearly zero.

Sadly, the recruit that enters a school under the Prop 48 rules, works hard, stays away from the athletic program, makes his grades, and is ready for a scholarship still loses a year of eligibility. This is true even though that player entered the college on his own finances or on anything other than an athletic scholarship. You have to be really motivated to work that hard to get your grades up and then be told you lose a year of your athletic prowess. There have been moves to alter this rule to get back that fourth year of eligibility, but it's still up in the air. Basically, all college athletes have five years to complete four years of eligibility.

Recently, high school and JUCO recruits engaged in a bit of "sandbagging" when it came down to ACT or SAT test scores. Many players, despite pleas from academic counselors and coaches, refused to take the tests until the last possible minute. In this way, the players used test scores as a type of "bargaining chip" in recruiting discussions. If a team showed interest, they would have to prove "loyalty" to the player by signing them without a test score. With precious few scholarships to give and top ranked players on the line, sandbagging on test scores could be an expensive proposition. The NCAA corrected that loophole in 1991, when they created a rule stating that a player must have taken the ACT or SAT *before* they could take an official visit to any school. If a school has to reveal everything to the player, the player should reciprocate and level with the officials and coaches about test scores, which greatly affects recruiting eligibility and recruiting costs.

When it comes down to Signing Day, Oh Boy, get those manuals out! There is a 48-hour dead period prior to 8:00 A.M. on Signing Day. That means that no recruit can be contacted by the school in any way just before the letter-of-intent can be signed. In the pre-1981 reform days, the head coach or an assistant could go to where the player lived and sign him in person. Today, the player must fax, mail or express mail the letter-of-intent back to the school.

This "Fax and FedEx" rule, which has been mentioned previously, and the "dead" periods are to prevent "kidnapping." Kidnapping in recruiting has a different meaning than in the criminal codes. Rather, this is the ancient and often-used practice of coaches "hiding out" recruits from rival college coaches. If the other teams couldn't find 'em, they couldn't sign 'em! The most common excuse used for a kidnapped player is that "he was out squirrel hunting!" Yeah, right! Most college coaches who have been in the business for any length of time can tell you some pretty good kidnapping stories. It is an illegal practice that has been wiped out thanks to NCAA rules. The whole idea behind these regulations is for the recruit to make a voluntary, knowing, and intelligent decision as to where he wants to obtain his higher education while helping the athletic team [win a national championship.]

It should be noted here that the NCAA has been under a legal siege since the early 1980s about its rules, regulations, and rights. The NCAA, Jerry "Tark the Shark" Tarkanian, and the University of Nevada at Las Vegas (the UNLV Runnin' Rebels) have been in litigation in some form or fashion for almost 20 years. Tark no longer coaches at UNLV, and it's small wonder why. Tark's case even went up to the United States Supreme Court, which sent the whole ugly mess back down. Tark and his program were accused, in several different years, of recruiting violations and providing "extra benefits" to his players. The administration at UNLV went so far as to install secret cameras in the basketball gyms on campus to catch Tark conducting illegal practices before they could legally start in November.

Books have been written about UNLV vs. the NCAA, but what may have really prompted the NCAA to open fire on the big programs may have been the battle over the rights to televise college football. For years, the NCAA controlled what you watched on TV concerning college football games. The NCAA, similar to a feudal lord, contended it owned the rights to college football telecasts and dictated policy accordingly.

In the middle of the 1980s, the universities of Oklahoma and Georgia sued the NCAA for colleges to be able to negotiate their own rights to TV and cable networks. The legal battle was long and protracted, but, in the end, the NCAA lost its TV rights. College conferences such as the SEC banded their members together and the CFA (College Football Association), was formed to help negotiate and deal their way through the network and cable maze. The legal action paid off as the average viewer can watch college football on fall Saturdays from 10:00 A.M. till 1 or 2:00 A.M. on Sunday if you catch it right with east and west coast games. One could argue that this action opened the doors for TV overexposure and saturation, but you don't hear fans and alumni complaining.

Depending on which side your bread is buttered, the current college football TV glut is cussed or praised. The actions of Georgia and Oklahoma were landmark and removed the "TV fiefdom" from NCAA clutches. Next on the horizon is the controversial notion of pay-per-view, although several teams, LSU most notable, have had some form of pay-per-view packages for years.

Call it a coincidence if you will, but shortly after the NCAA lost this case and the TV rights to the teams, the enforcement division seemed to pick up the pace on NCAA investigations and probations. Oklahoma paid the price for a number of violations in the late '80s, causing the departure of longtime coach Barry Switzer and Georgia was investigated, but nothing came of it. Georgia was eventually throttled in a lawsuit by English professor Jan Kemp, and the result of the ruling of that case in Georgia brought sweeping academic reform to the Bulldog athletic department.

The NCAA went after high-profile teams and schools that were once considered off-limits for investigation. The Kentucky Wildcat basketball team, one of the most hallowed programs in the nation, was placed on a two-year probation when an express mail package was accidentally opened en route to a recruit and cash money popped out. The *Lexington Herald-Leader* won the Pulitzer Prize for its investigation on this one.

Nearly every Southwest Conference football team also landed on probation by the NCAA in the late 1980s. Too many recruiting violations put teams such as Texas A&M in hot water and the SWC suffered horrible publicity. The cause of all of this was probably the intense recruiting wars in talent rich Texas, but, surely the NCAA would not have been looking so closely if they hadn't been stung so much in court on the TV issue.

These days, the list of glamorous schools with big programs under NCAA scrutiny is truly amazing. Programs at Washington, Texas A&M, Alabama, Oklahoma, Tennessee, and Auburn were once considered to be untouchable, but the long arm of the NCAA continues to reach out and touch some big money programs. The primary target continues to be the "out-of-control" boosters or the big money alumni. Some of these so-called boosters couldn't care less about scandal, probation and the loss of coaching personnel as long as the bowl bids, wins over arch rivals, and national championship aspirations continue.

Recently, the NCAA has beaten back challenges to its procedures arising out of the enforcement division. Various state legislatures have gotten creative with laws designed to circumvent or alter the NCAA rules. The state of Nebraska tried to classify all collegiate athletes under their worker's compensation laws. They argued that since the players receive a scholarship and are unpaid workers on behalf of the school, they should be compensated in case of injuries. The Nebraska legislature wisely voted that ridiculous notion down, but other states are following Nebraska's lead.

The state of Kansas, home of the NCAA at the town of Mission, recently launched a due process attack at the organization. Kansas, stung by some of its colleges such as Wichita State and Kansas being put on NCAA probation, sought to have laws passed to curb the NCAA's investigative tactics and force them to follow due process accords provided by the U.S. Constitution. In effect, Kansas wanted to hold the NCAA Enforcement Section to follow procedures afforded to criminal defendants.

In an ultimate show of powerful arrogance, the NCAA told the Kansas legislators, in no uncertain terms, that if those laws passed and went into effect, then they would declare all Kansas colleges and universities who were NCAA members to be ineligible for NCAA competition. Facing an unbelievable flight to the smaller and less prestigious NAIA, the Kansas crew backed off—for now.

The NCAA can even have a chilling effect on the First Amendment to the United States Constitution—the right to free speech. The organization already has several rules and regulations preventing coaches from revealing which players they are recruiting and the recruiting process in general. The NCAA rules are built to prevent "unfair advantage," which is the all-purpose catch phrase these days. It is argued by the higher-ups that many programs, such as Notre Dame football and Kentucky basketball, enjoy such a high profile and a glut of publicity that if their coaches spoke out about recruits, then the smaller schools with lower profiles would not be able to generate the same news and interest about their recruits.

This rule is constantly broken and it can cost the violator. Take Georgia basketball coach Hugh Durham, for example. Several years ago, the peppery Durham was being interviewed on powerful WSB 750 AM in Atlanta during basketball recruiting and he inadvertently got carried away and mentioned the name of a blue-chip player committing to the Dawgs. After the NCAA stepped in, Georgia could no longer pursue that particular recruit and Hugh had to be a lot more careful about divulging recruiting information to the press. No matter that Coach Durham, as an American citizen, has the right of free speech. He is a subject of the NCAA kingdom by virtue of his pay-check from Georgia as hoops coach , therefore he has placed himself under that control of his free speech. The NCAA even rules and directs what types of endorsement contracts, mostly with the shoe companies, that coaches like Durham can sign. In fact, they have to report publicly to their school how much money they make and what type of endorsements they have on hand. So much for free speech and freedom of individuals to privacy and to contract for personal gain.

In the late 1980s, several specialty publications devoted to reporting on the athletics news of certain SEC schools ran afoul of the NCAA and its curtailing of free speech. The tabloids, most of which are independent of university control but dependent on the athletic department's cooperation, began what was known as "Operation Saturation." The purpose of these projects was to have subscribers or generous benefactors purchase a subscription to publications such as *Tiger Rag,* (LSU), *Cats' Pause* (Kentucky), the *Ole Miss Spirit,* and *Gator Bait* (Florida Gators), and donate the publications to a local high school so students and, especially, student-athletes could have access to the magazines at their high school libraries.

The publications printed up a checklist of the high schools and each time a donated subscription was purchased, the high school would be checked off and the subscription would be placed in the name of the high school's library. "Operation Saturation" was obviously designed to get those magazines in the hands of students, athletes and non-athletes, and promote the school through the magazines. In Louisiana and Florida, "Operation Saturation" was off to a flying start and had just started to kick in in Mississippi when, Guess Who?, the NCAA stepped in.

The guys and gals from Mission, Kansas went to the schools connected with these specialty publications and told them that their athletic programs could be in NCAA hot water and face probation because of "Operation Saturation." Citing the unfair advantage rules, the NCAA asked the schools to help cease the program, mainly because schools that did not have such publicity ties could not "saturate" high schools with this type of info flow and high-profile "advertisement." Never mind that most of these publications have separate staffs, separate companies, separate interests, and are not subject to those "representative of athletic interests rules." Because of unfair media coverage, the NCAA told the athletic officials that "Operation Saturation" had to go.

Being dependent on the schools for information and being extremely loyal to the programs, the specialty publications, voluntarily and at the schools' requests, ended "Operation Saturation." In doing so, however, each editor involved fired off a scathing editorial about

58

the role of the NCAA and the dampening of the publication's First Amendment rights.. After all, these publications were having not only their free speech limited, but they were actually losing business, money, and the goodwill generated by "Operation Saturation" in the high school hallways. This could have been easily interpreted as intentional interference with business relations, although supposedly no malice was directed towards the magazines . Once again, the NCAA had successfully silenced free speech, and this time it reached persons and businesses that in no way could be considered under the organization's direct influence and control.

It should be noted here that the U.S. Supreme Court and various federal and state courts have repeatedly ruled that the NCAA is a *voluntary* organization and that the rules they operate under are set by the members. These rulings make it clear that the NCAA's operating manual can pass legal challenges and the organization can effectively bypass rules and regulations centered on due process considerations. The main idea here is that when you voluntarily joined the NCAA, you forfeited rights you are guaranteed in any other business in America.

With the courts being held at bay, the next challenge the NCAA must hold off regarding their rules will come from the U.S. Congress. There has been activity in the House of Representatives and the U.S. Senate of late that indicates that disgruntled constituents have gotten the ears of legislators to do something about the NCAA investigatory tactics.

The "victims" of the NCAA probes claim that they do not have the right of cross examination of accusers, no right to a full and complete investigation process to discover the NCAA allegations, no right to a full-blown hearing with witnesses and the like, and the reliance of the Infractions Committee on hearsay, rumors, and third-hand information. In fact, when an NCAA investigation is launched against a college these days, that college better promptly conduct its own investigation of the charges or face further wrath from the NCAA that they "lack institutional control." The penalties can be higher if the school does not try to find out what is going on and merely answers the NCAA charges with a "no comment" or "We deny everything."

The shape of the NCAA is mainly in the hands of the presidents, chancellors, and CEOs of the member schools. The President's Commission is considered to be the most powerful influence on the

NCAA guidelines and rules. Despite the cry and hue of the coaches and athletic directors, it is the presidents that set the tone for NCAA conventions and what happens to programs. To add to all of these woes, the U.S. government, under Title IX of the United States Code, is looking to genderize NCAA athletic programs. Gender-based equity is the latest challenge to the power of the NCAA and the future of NCAA athletic programs.

This particular challenge will cut to the quick of athletic budgets if implemented to the fullest. Gender based equity will seek to equalize funding for certain athletic programs. Mainly, these types of lawsuits will go for the football jugular and cut out unnecessary spending by the large programs. The legal noise will be for more funds and more women's programs to be created. Notre Dame is the greatest example of a Title IX problem in several years. The Fighting Irish were hit with a Title IX lawsuit and had to make some concessions to women's athletics some time ago.

A federal judge in 1992 ordered Division II Indiana University out of Pennsylvania to reinstate several women's athletic programs that the school had cut due to economics. Using Title IX "legalese", the court said that the school had high-profile teams in football and basketball that made money. By reinstating the programs, the school, according to the court, was providing required services to the rest of the student body. If this tiny little Division II school is judicially proclaimed to have a high profile in football and basketball, imagine what could happen to other larger programs that ignore funding for women's sports.

Brown University, an Ivy League athletic powerhouse, was forced to reinstate women's programs thanks to a 1993 court ruling. The school was ordered to bring back two women's sports, but not two men's programs, all of which were cut because the school had no money to run the programs. So much for cost cutting, NCAA!

Of late, the NCAA may be taking steps to police itself and to streamline all of the procedures that players, coaches, fans, alumni and athletic directors have complained about for years. The President's Commission is poised to introduce open and public hearings before the Infractions Committee, appoint special hearing officers, and allow schools and NCAA investigators to submit to certain stipulations and agree to submit uncontested items to the Mission moguls. This would

60

really speed up the lengthy process of an NCAA inquiry and possibly eliminate the loud noise over due process violations. (Right now, it averages over a year between the time the NCAA launches an investigation until the case is concluded.) If they can resolve these "new" concepts with the privacy acts regarding the flow of information from college and high school students, then look for drastic changes in the investigative machine of the NCAA.

But before you think the dark side of recruiting collegiate athletics may be seeing some light, consider some of the most outrageous, but true, recruiting tales of them all.

*****

Roosevelt Potts is a talented football player with one of the most checkered pasts of any NCAA player. At age 12, his father was sentenced to seven years in jail. At age 13, his mother passed away as a result of a heart attack. Potts then moved in with his grandmother, but then she died when Roosevelt was a super sophomore in high school in Rayville, Louisiana. Potts, after these tragedies, lived alone in Rayville, a town that, according to him, still has racial problems.

Potts was one of the best running backs in the history of Rayville High School and was being highly recruited. His future, despite a tragic past, was looking up. He would probably be a Prop 48 player and have to sit out a year because of academics, but he could make a great name for himself and rise out of the ashes of a disadvantaged past.

Then, one night at a local bar in Rayville, Potts was, according to him, cornered by white men and he was placed into a "kill-or-be-killed" situation. Roosevelt says that he fired a gun into the air inside the bar and that his friend shot at the crowd of white tormentors. People were hurt, but no one was killed, and Potts was carted off to jail on one count of aggravated assault. He entered a plea of guilty to the charge and was facing sentencing in Louisiana as a result of his plea.

All of this boiled over during recruiting time. Potts' choices came down to Ole Miss and Northeast Louisiana, located in Monroe. This was Billy Brewer's territory and he knew this area of Louisiana well. He had contacts due to his coaching stint at Louisiana Tech and he really wanted to sign Potts, who could be an impact running back. The Rebels received a verbal commitment from Roosevelt. Although he would be a Prop 48 player, he told the Ole Miss staff and Billy Brewer that he would sign a letter of intent with Ole Miss.

On Signing Day in February, 1989, Potts signed with Northeast Louisiana and not with the Rebels. Billy Brewer was livid. Ole Miss fans claimed that the local judge handling Potts' case was pressured by Northeast alumni and supporters to hold Potts' possible sentence over his head if he didn't sign with the Indians. It was said that he would surely go to jail if he went out of state to Ole Miss. Talk about the ultimate recruiting pressure!

Potts received a suspended sentence and had to pay one-third of two victims' medical bills. He was also put on five years supervised probation, meaning that he was under limited conditions of living and had to report to a probation officer. He was allowed to complete high school and he went to Monroe as a Prop 48 player. He became an All-American running back in the Southland Conference and almost declared himself eligible for the 1992 NFL draft. He was only 762 yards shy of Northeast's all-time rushing record in only two years of eligibility. He played in the 1993 Senior Bowl and was drafted by the pros.

Billy Brewer later took back his words about what the judge did in sentencing Roosevelt. After all, there would be other recruits from the area that the Rebs would want and you just don't burn bridges, especially with a judge, in recruiting wars. To this day, however, most Ole Miss followers of recruiting will tell you that a jail sentence, of all things, was used to sign a player away from another team.

Chuck Rounsaville of the *Ole Miss Spirit* called Potts' high school coach the night after Potts had committed. Here is the exact conversation as it appeared in the February 18, 1989, edition of the *Spirit*:

Coach: (Whispering, obviously nervous) Coach, these judges and stuff over here aren't going to let this kid leave the state....

Chuck: Wait a minute, I'm not a coach, I'm with the press...

Coach: (Voice raised) THE PRESS, OH, MY.....

Chuck: Wait a minute, I 'm friendly press. I do the Ole Miss athletic paper. Is something wrong?...

Coach: I can't talk about it now, but yes, something's wrong.

As Chuck then wrote, "End of conversation, end of Mr . Potts being a Rebel."

As the name of this chapter implies, there is a dark side to recruiting. Name another situation in the history of college recruiting in any sport where a student-athlete was subjected to losing his freedom if he didn't sign with a certain school. Rattle off all of the kidnappings, the lies, the double dealings, the money being spread around, the new cars and women being offered, and you still fall way short in the saga of Roosevelt Potts.

You may read about Roosevelt in the NFL, as he was drafted by the Indianapolis Colts in 1993, but you'll never read about how he became a Northeast Louisiana Indian thanks to the criminal justice system being spun for a recruiting loop!

*****

On February 5, 1992, an athletically talented high school quarterback named Ike Wilson out of New Orleans, signed a letter-of-intent with Mississippi State under head coach Jackie Sherrill.

On August 10, 1992, Ike Wilson stood before District Judge Joseph F. Grefer in Gretna, Louisiana, Jefferson Parish, in an orange and white striped Nautica shirt hanging outside of his blue jeans. Ike entered a plea of guilty to one count of cocaine distribution. He was sentenced by Judge Grefer to five years of hard labor in the Louisiana Department of Corrections, but all of those years were suspended and he was placed on two years probation. Judge Grefer ordered the signal caller to lose 30 days of his driving privilege, to pay $1,000 of restitution to the Jefferson Parish Sheriff's Office, to pay a $300 fine plus all costs of court and $20 a month to the probation office. If he completes his probation, he can be adjudged not guilty by the court and clean up his record somewhat.

A three-member admissions committee from Mississippi State now had to take up his case. Should he or should he not be allowed to enroll in the Starkville school to play football for Jackie Sherrill?

Ike Wilson grew up in the West Bank suburbs of New Orleans, an area infested with drugs, crime ,and despair. Ike's parents, however, are hard workers. His mom works for the bar association, ironically, and his dad is employed by an oil rig supply company. Ike is 18 and he has a 19-year-old brother and a 16-year-old sister.

Yet, this pigskin tosser has been in three different high schools, has a history of problems with juvenile authorities, and was accused of being involved in all types of criminal activity. Some of which was true and some of it untrue.

The *Clarion Ledger*, court documents, and Jefferson County

63

District Attorney's office profiled Ike Wilson in a Mike Knobler article dated August 11, 1992. It reads like this:

April 5, 1991—Wilson commits simple battery allegedly with a tire iron and criminal damage to property less than $500.

August 1, 1991—Sells one ounce of cocaine to an undercover policeman.

October 30, 1991—Pleads guilty to simple battery and criminal damage that occurred April 5. Sentenced to 100 hours of community service, six months in jail suspended, six months probation. Ordered to pay $215 restitution.

January 10, 1992, 4:30 P.M.. thru January 12, 1992, 6:00 P.M..—Jailed for failure to appear.

February 5, 1992—Signs letter-of-intent with Miss. State.

March 20, 1992—Arrested and eventually charged with one count of cocaine distribution, one count of conspiracy to injure public records, and probation violation.

April 10, 1992 thru July 27, 1992—Jailed on Fridays at 6 P.M.. until Sundays at 8 P.M.

July 27, 1992—House arrest with two hours of community service and one and one half hour to work out.

July 30, 1992—Released from house arrest and ordered to perform eight hours community service.

August 10, 1992—Pleads guilty to August 1, 1991, count of cocaine distribution. Other charges dismissed. Those other charges included one count of cocaine distribution and one count of conspiracy to injure public records.

In addition to all of this, Ike's case had originally been brought to public attention when he was allegedly involved in an armed robbery in New Orleans. No armed robbery or robbery charges were filed against him in his celebrated arrest.

Ike had also been tossed out of three high schools for having in his possession a beeper or pager. In case you are not up to speed, drug dealers frequently carry around beepers or pagers for the purposes of "customer service." Normal high school students just don't carry around beepers or pagers.

Wilson was recruited primarily by Pete Jenkins, who had been on the LSU staff before joining Jackie Sherrill at Miss. State. Sherrill visited Wilson and had him wrapped up to sign a letter-of-intent. When he signed in February, 1992, Sherrill did not know that the talented QB was on probation for the battery charge that he pleaded guilty to less than one month before Signing Day.

On Wednesday, August 12, 1992, Dennis Smith, news editor for WLBT-TV in Jackson, Mississippi, delivered an editorial ripping Miss. State officials for even considering allowing Wilson to enroll. Smith described the decision a "no-brainer" and wondered why the panel even had to meet to check out this matter. Smith also publicly wondered what kind of signal Miss. State was sending out to incoming freshmen if they allowed Ike Wilson to play football in Starkville.

When the three-member panel for the Bulldogs admissions met in August, Wilson's scholarship offer was apparently rejected. No official word was announced and no State officials would confirm the alleged decision.

Ike Wilson enrolled at Northeastern Oklahoma A&M in August, 1992. In a September 3, 1992, edition of the *Commercial Appeal* out of Memphis, Tennessee, Ike Wilson defended his character with the following statement: "One thing to look at is the ratio of how many times they tried to get me and how many times they got me."

Jackie Sherrill could recruit Ike Wilson once again out of the JUCO ranks to play quarterback for Miss. State.

Seven games into the 1992 NEO football season, however, Ike Wilson was dismissed from the football team for reasons not disclosed.

*****

Wednesday, December 16, 1992, was a special day in the lives of 1,079 senior young men and women at the Eaves Memorial Coliseum on the campus of Auburn University. It was Commencement Day—a day when college students became college graduates and entered the real world. Most Commencement Days are happy, yet solemn and pompous ceremonies marked in tradition with caps and gowns and families and photographers and professors with fancy robes presenting degrees to long lines of hopefuls. Surely you have all heard of "Pomp and Circumstance."

But on this day at Auburn, there was one man and his wife receiving degrees that had arrived and would leave with police escorts. She would receive her degree in communications. He would earn a degree, oddly enough, in criminal justice.

He would be the first of this pair to receive his sheepskin. When he approached the middle of the stage, the crowd in attendance—those 1,079 seniors and another 2,500 spectators, began to make a boisterous noise. When Eric Ramsey, former Auburn football player, reached his destination to collect his degree, the crowd booed loudly and clear shouts of "Go to Hell!" from the Auburn students and supporters were aimed at him. Some of the students had the words "BOO ERIC" taped on top of their mortarboard caps.

Ramsey, former defensive back for the Tigers, had ratted on his school. In fact, he brought down the house that had given him a scholarship. Years earlier, Ramsey, for some strange reason, had tape-recorded conversations with assistant football coaches and head coach Pat Dye of the Auburn Tigers. These tapes contained proof of illegal recruiting activity and extra benefits given to Ramsey. These extra benefits included cash and steaks given to the college gridder by an Auburn booster as arranged by Dye and by assistant coaches. Ramsey had left Auburn early in hopes of being a professional football player in the NFL.

After he had been cut by the Kansas City Chiefs, a bitter Ramsey released the tapes to the media and then to the NCAA. Almost a year later in 1992, the NCAA sent Auburn a formal letter of inquiry, the major step towards probation and/or sanctions by the organization. In the letter of inquiry, the NCAA stated that Auburn head football coach and then athletic director Pat Dye knew about these extra benefits in violation of NCAA rules and that there was a "lack of institutional control" at the Auburn athletic department.

That last allegation is the devastating one. When the NCAA hits a program with "lack of institutional control," that means that probation and heavy sanctions are sure to follow. In the wake of this NCAA probe, Auburn head coach Pat Dye resigned on November 15, 1992, days before Thanksgiving and the annual Alabama-Auburn Iron Bowl game in Birmingham won by the Tide 17-0. Pat Dye had created a massive program in his tenure at Auburn and his Tiger football teams were the SEC team of the 1980s with four SEC crowns. Under his reign as A.D., the Auburn athletic programs had grown to be one of the premiere programs in the South and in the country cranking out millions in revenues for the school.

One football player and his cassette tapes had wrecked the castle. The fans and followers of Auburn, fiercely loyal to their school, erupted when Ramsey's name was called. Ramsey walked off stage pumping his fists in the air in a jeering mock motion to the crowd which brought on more boos. When Ramsey's wife Twilitta followed him moments later, she was booed just as loudly and lustily as Eric had been. The couple then hugged on stage and Twilitta Ramsey made an obscene hand gesture to the heckling thousands. (Translated: She flipped them off!)

Eric and Twilitta Ramsey, newly graduated, walked out of Eaves Memorial Coliseum arm-in-arm and left under police escort. He arrived as a student-athlete at Auburn several years ago by way of a scholarship bestowed upon him in the recruiting process. The school had given him his chance to earn that degree in criminal justice. He repaid them with scandal, shame, resignation of a veteran football coach, and the eminent disarray of that same athletic program.

When is the last time any of you reading this saw someone getting booed and heckled for receiving a college degree?

Folks, this recruiting stuff is serious!

*****

On Wednesday, January 13, 1993, Shelton Hand, the attorney for Mississippi College at Clinton, Mississippi, held a press conference to explain the school's position on the harshest NCAA penalty ever placed on an in-state school. Hand met the sports media at the MC School of Law in Jackson in a law classroom similar to a jury box.

This tiny Division II school had just been stripped of the 1989 National Football Championship won by the Choctaws on a snowy field 3-0 in Florence, Alabama, against Jacksonville State. MC had won this title on the field, but the NCAA wiped the title from the record books. For having double the allowed number of football players on scholarships, this private elitist Baptist college, the oldest one established in Mississippi, was suffering through its worst moment in athletics. A four-year probation, loss of scholarships, off-campus recruiting bans, and severe sanctions were tossed in for good measure. These penalties were a lot tougher than those ever tossed on the "Big Three" of Ole Miss, State, and Southern.

The MC president, Lewis Nobles, regularly does not return phone calls related to the school's athletic department and he placed gag orders on all employees and persons involved in this controversy. He

67

has not, and probably will not, provide one word of explanation for this shameful incident in Mississippi athletics. How could this have happened?

How could a small school not spot this problem through administrative controls? Why did it take 13 months to discover the extra number of scholarships?

Rick Cleveland, sports editor of the *Clarion Ledger* asked the obvious question: "If I'm a sports editor and the newspaper is allowing me 20 positions on my staff, it wouldn't take very long for the editor to determine that I had 40 working. How could it take so long?"

MC Attorney Hand responded: "How long does it take the U.S. to do something about Saddam Hussein?"

"That's apples and oranges," responded Cleveland.

"I like both," said Hand.

End of press conference and end of any kind of humilty that should attach itself to this so-called institution of high integrity and learning.

*****

When the "Big Three" of Mississippi got hit by the NCAA with probation penalties, boosters of all three schools were involved. Miss. State boosters provided free clothing to Larry Gillard. Ole Miss boosters provided transportation and paid for high school players to attend Ole Miss summer football camp plus booster Charles Gates was banned from being too close to the program. Southern Miss. boosters were involved in payments to players and one of their boosters was implicated in the USM probe.

Compared to what boosters of the SMU program did to get the Mustangs the death penalty, the involvement of these rabid Mississippi boosters seems like small minnows in a very large pond filled with whales. But it really doesn't take much to get a multimillion dollar college football program in trouble with the NCAA.

In an effort to shed light on the dark side of recruiting, here is a guide to the do's and don'ts of boosters involved with their schools:

What is a booster? Under NCAA rules, a booster is defined as follows: "A promoter of your institution's athletic program who is known (or who should have been known) by a member of your institution's executive or athletics administration to have engaged in any of the following activities:

—Participated in or been a member of an agency or organization promoting your institution's intercollegiate athletics program;

—Contributed financially to your athletics department or to your institution's athletics booster organization;

—Helped recruit prospects, even if you or your institution did not request assistance;

—Assisted in providing benefits to enrolled student-athletes or their families, or

—Promoted your institution's athletics program in other ways."

Once identified as a booster, an individual always keeps that identity. In other words, Once A Booster, Always A Booster. (Source: *NCAA Guide to Recruiting 1992-93,* page 6, Bylaw 13.02.10.1)

You can see that the definition of a booster by the NCAA is certainly broad and can easily be interpreted against both the person or persons involved and the school. Now that you know what you are, here is what you can and cannot do:

Do: Attend whatever booster education seminar or program your school sponsors or promotes. Knowing the rules and hearing them from your own athletic officials seems to have more effect and meaning.

Don't: Become involved in recruiting activities of any nature or type.

Do: Support your school financially because your contributions help recruiting budgets.

Don't: Make in-person, on- or-off campus recruiting contacts with prospects.

Do: Make yourself aware of NCAA rules as they apply to boosters. Read on and we'll save you the trouble of buying the rules.

Don't: Write or telephone prospects, their relatives, or legal guardians.

Do: Speak to prospects on the telephone *only* if the prospect calls you and no recruiting occurs on the phone.

Don't: Contact prospects' coaches, principals, or counselors in an attempt to evaluate prospects.

Do: Refer all questions posed to you by a prospect about your athletic program to your athletic department staff. In other words, call the coach!

Don't: Visit prospects' schools to pick up transcripts or films pertaining to evaluation of the prospects' academic or athletics ability.

Do: Attend prospects' games or contests on your own. Besides, this gives you an advantage in seeing the player and provides you with a preview of his or her talents. It also gives you the chance to at least talk semi-intelligently during recruiting conversations with fellow crazies.

Don't: Contact prospects at these games or contests.

Do: Contact the prospect if you are a longtime friend and/or neighbor of the prospect. After all, let's not be ridiculous about all of this. People still have to live with each other!

Don't: Contact the prospect for any recruiting purposes even if the prospect is a longtime friend and/or neighbor and this is especially true if a coach asks you to speak to the prospect.

Do: Consult your athletic department or the coaching staff if you even believe an activity may be improper or illegal. Let them get a ruling from the NCAA or their conference before something new arises.

Don't: Provide transportation for a prospect to your school's games or practices either on an official or unoffiial visit.

Do: Know when a prospect becomes a prospect officially under NCAA rules. This happens on July 1 after the athlete finishes his or her junior year in high school. Exceptions are made of members of athletic staffs at the military academies.

Don't: Provide a prospect with a highlight film or recruiting videotape in any form or fashion.

Do: Participate in any pickup basketball games or other similar activities with prospects—just make sure no recruiting goes on during these spontaneous and incidental activities.

Don't: Deliberately arrange any of the above just to curry recruiting favor. In other words, don't be phony.

Do: Assist any or all players who have signed national Letters-of-Intent with your school in arranging or discussing summer employment.

Don't: Do any of the above until that letter-of-intent is signed!

Do: Assist your school in providing any testimonials or presentations for recruiting videotapes as long as the presentation is generic and not tailor-made for particular individuals.

Do: Insist that your school have a "contact person" for the purposes of answering any recruiting questions on a day-to-day basis. Usually, the recruiting coordinator at your school should be set up for this function.

The bottom line on this list of Do's and Don'ts: if you have any questions about any activities of boosters, whether they involve you or someone else, call your school immediately and bring them to the institution's attention.

It's the only way to help avoid the Dark Side of recruiting.

CHAPTER 6

The National Letter
of Intent

Q UICK, A RECRUITING riddle: What's 4 pages long,
complicated as all get-out, and is the most highly sought
after piece of paper in the month of February?
Answer: The National Letter of Intent!

Many years ago this document never existed. Colleges just invited
prospects onto their campuses and the athletes just signed up for
scholarships. As the NCAA rules took shape, the National Letter of
Intent, which is shortened to the NLI, was developed. Early NLIs were
simple forms, one pagers and no-brainers.

Time and the complicated nature of NCAA rulings in the 1980s
took care of the old fashioned NLI. In fact, the NLI is now *the only*
manner to sign up college athletic prospects. Prior to the current form
of the NLI, many athletes had to sign two letters-of-intent, one national
and one for the conference of the school. (See Chapter 5, The Dark
Side, p.52.)

For example, an athlete recruited by an SEC team would face two
separate Signing Days instead of just one. In recruiting days of yore,
the typical SEC football signee would sign on in December for football
with an SEC letter-of-intent and then sign the NLI in January or
February. When the player singed the conference letter-of-intent, the
rest of the conference could no longer seek his signature, but the player
could still sing with any other school outside of the conference with
the NLI, considered the actual binding instrument of recruiting.

When the NCAA consolidated the football Signing Day, the
practice of separate Signing Wars within conferences disappeared.
Now, everybody fights for the NLI, which has involved into a legally
binding and critical piece of paper.

Through the assistance of the offices of the Legislative Services of the NCAA and the Collegiate Commissioners Association, this book is presenting an actual NLI used in 1992 and it is reprinted in its entirety. This chapter will focus on the meaning of the words and phrases contained in the NLI and how it affects the average recruit. Not many people are allowed the opportunity to view an actual NLI, so this is a true recruiting treat.

In the Did You Know? Department, the NLI is administered by the CCA, or the Collegiate Commissioners Association. The form is updated each year with NCAA signing dates. The CCA is in charge of the NLI annually on some type of rotating basis. Did you also know that this NLI has to be renewed each and every year of the athlete's eligibility? Not many recruiting buffs know this little tidbit, but the NCAA rules dictate the renewal which is usually automatically granted if eligibility for the athlete is OK.

The actual content of the NLI has always been a mystery for recruiting fans. There are stiff penalties for the athlete that does not know what the words mean. If an athlete does not attend the school he or she signs with for one full academic year and then enrolls in another school, that athlete cannot participate in the athletic programs of the new school for two full academic years of residence. In addition, the athlete loses two years of eligibility if this scenario plays out and the athlete jumps ship.

The NLI goes on to explain the financial aid guarantee in writing. Upon signing of the NLI, the athlete is provided financial aid, but remember, those scholarship documents are completely separate from the NLI and are usually signed when the athlete arrives on campus and is ready to enroll for classes. The document then goes on the spell out that if the athlete signs a pro contract, the athlete is still bound by the NLI even if the school cannot give him or her financial aid under NCAA rules as a result of the pro status. That's the equivalent of athletic limbo.

Next comes the Null and Void section where the NLI tells you when the NLI is thrown out the window. The obvious terms deal with eligibility and those terms are right out of the NCAA guidelines. Next on the list is the one year absence clause where an athlete basically abandons the NLI if the athlete does not attend that particular school. This is the reason Prop 48 players frequently have to re-sign an NLI.

If an athlete joins the Armed Forces or a church mission, wave bye-

bye to the NLI. Ditto if the sport you signed up for is discontinued. Finally, and this one is rich, if the school violates NCAA or conference rules while recruiting the player, the NLI is declared Null and Void. Now, obviously, this little trick doesn't surface until the NCAA or conference appeals for eligibility restoration have been completed, which could last until the next century making the whole point of this clause rather ridiculous. The recruit involved probably will be in the pros or in the real world before most of this happens with the current speed of NCAA investigations.

The NLI provides for a mutual release system in the event the parties part. The interesting section involved in this portion of the NLI states that a coach is not authorized to void, cancel or grant a release and that a release of the NLI cannot be conditional or selective. Only one valid NLI is allowed and the athlete cannot sign more than one NLI. (Who would want to?)

Of course, after the athlete signs the NLI, all conferences and schools must respect the signing and back off all recruiting efforts aimed towards that athlete. If other schools keep recruiting the player, the athlete is required to notify any recruiter that he has signed the NLI. A falsification clause is added on the NLI to prevent fraud on the part of the athlete. Neither party can add or subtract anything to the NLI as it is a document that stands alone with no side deals. The document must be unchanged in this issued form.

Deadlines are important to the NLI. First, there is a 14 day period where parents or legal guardians must sign the NLI after the date the NLI issued. If it is not signed in this two week period, the NLI is worthless, but another NLI can be issued. Secondly, the NLI has to be filed with the conference by the school within three weeks after the date of the final signature on the NLI. If not filed in this time frame, again, the NLI is no good, but, again, another NLI can be issued if need be.

The NLI has an Official Time for Validity. This time means that the NLI is considered to be officially signed on the final date of the signature by the athlete or his or her parents or guardians. If no time of day is listed, it is presumed by the NLI that the time was ll:59 P.M. With this in mind, do the athletes turn into recruiting pumpkins at Midnight?

Finally, an appeals procedure is outlined by the NLI plus a four year

1992 NATIONAL LETTER OF INTENT (NLI)

Administered by the Collegiate Commissioners Association (CCA)

Do not sign prior to **8:00 a.m.** on the following initial signing dates, or after the final date listed for each sport.

	Sport	Initial Signing Date	Final Signing Date
_____	Basketball (Early Period)	November 13, 1991	November 20, 1991
_____	Basketball (Late Period)	April 15, 1992	May 15, 1992
_____	Football, Midyear JC Transfer	December 11, 1991	January 15, 1992
_____	Football (Regular Period)	February 5, 1992	April 1, 1992
_____	Women's Volleyball, Field Hockey, Soccer, Water Polo	February 5, 1992	August 1, 1992
_____	All Other Sports (Early Period)	November 13, 1991	November 20, 1991
_____	All Other Sports (Late Period)	April 15, 1992	August 1, 1992

(Place an "x" on the proper line above.)

Name of Prospect _____
Type Proper Name, Including Middle Name or Initial

Address _____
Street Number   City, State, Zip Code

Submission of this NLI has been authorized by:

SIGNED _____   _____   _____
Director of Athletics   Date Issued to Prospect   Sport (men's/women's)

This is to certify my decision to enroll at _____
Name of Institution

```
IMPORTANT - READ CAREFULLY

It is important to read carefully this entire document before signing it in triplicate. One
copy is to be retained by you and two copies are to be returned to the institution, one
of which will be filed with the appropriate conference commissioner.
```

1. **Initial Enrollment in Four-Year Institution.** This NLI is applicable only to prospective student-athletes who will be entering four-year institutions for the first time as fulltime students, except for "4-2-4" college transfers who are graduating from junior college as outlined in paragraph 7-b.

1

2. **Basic Penalty.** I understand that if I do not attend the institution named on page 1 for one full academic year, and enroll in another institution participating in the NLI program, I may not represent the latter institution in intercollegiate athletics competition until I have completed two full academic years of residence at the latter institution. Further, I understand that I will forfeit eligibility for two seasons of intercollegiate athletics competition in all sports except as otherwise provided in this Letter. This is in addition to any eligibility expended at the institution at which I initially enrolled.

   a. **Early Signing Period Penalties.** A prospective student-athlete who signs a National Letter of Intent during the early signing period (November 13-20, 1991) will be ineligible for practice and competition in football for a two-year period. A violation of this provision shall result in the loss of two seasons of competition in the sport of football.

3. **Financial Aid Requirement.** I must receive in writing an award or recommendation for athletics financial aid from the institution named on page 1 at the time of my signing for this NLI to be valid. The offer or recommendation shall list the terms and conditions of the award, including the amount and duration of the financial aid. If such recommended financial aid is not approved within the institution's normal time period for awarding financial aid, this NLI shall be invalid.

   a. **Professional Sports Contract.** If I sign a professional sports contract, I will remain bound by the provisions of this NLI even if the institution named on page 1 is prohibited from making athletically related financial aid available to me under NCAA rules.

4. **Provisions of Letter Satisfied.**

   a. **One-Year Attendance Requirement Met.** The terms of this NLI shall be satisfied if I attend the institution named on page 1 for at least one academic year (i.e., two full regular semesters or three full regular quarters).

   b. **Junior College Graduation.** The terms of this NLI shall be satisfied if I graduate from junior college after signing a NLI while in high school or during my first year in junior college.

5. **Letter Becomes Null and Void.** This NLI shall be declared null and void if any of the following occurs:

   a. **Admissions and Eligibility Requirements.** This NLI shall be declared null and void if the institution with which I signed notifies me in writing that I have been denied admission, or if I have not, by the institution's opening day of classes in the fall of 1992 (or, for a midyear junior college football signee, the opening day of its classes of the winter or spring term of 1992), met the institution's requirements for admission, its academic requirements for financial aid to athletes, the NCAA requirement for freshman financial aid (NCAA Bylaw 14.3) or the NCAA junior college transfer rule.

   (1) It is presumed that I am eligible for admission and financial aid until information is submitted to the contrary. Thus, it is mandatory for me to provide a transcript of my previous academic record and an application for admission to the institution named on page 1.

   (2) If I am eligible for admission, but the institution named on page 1 defers admission to a subsequent term, this NLI shall be rendered null and void. However, if I defer my admission, the NLI remains binding.

   (3) If I become a nonqualifier (applicable to NCAA Division I or II signees) or a partial qualifier (applicable only to NCAA Division I signees) as per NCAA Bylaw 14.3, this NLI shall be rendered null and void.

   (4) For a Midyear Junior College Football Transfer signee, the NLI remains binding for the following fall term if the prospect was eligible for admission and financial aid, and met the NCAA junior college transfer requirements for competition, for the winter or spring term, but chose to delay his admission.

2

b.   **One-Year Absence.** This NLI shall be null and void if I have not attended any institution (or attended an institution, including a junior college, that does not participate in the NLI Program) for at least one academic year after signing this NLI, provided my request for athletics financial aid for a subsequent fall term is not approved by the institution with which I signed. To receive this waiver, I must file with the appropriate conference commissioner a statement from the Director of Athletics at the institution named on page 1 that such financial aid will not be available to me for the requested fall term.

c.   **Service in U. S. Armed Forces, Church Mission.** This NLI will be null and void if I serve on active duty with the armed forces of the United States or on an official church mission for at least eighteen (18) months.

d.   **Discontinued Sport.** This NLI shall be null and void if my sport is discontinued by the institution named on page 1.

e.   **Recruiting Rules Violation.** If the institution (or a representative of its athletics interests) named on page 1 violates NCAA or conference rules while recruiting me, as found through the NCAA or conference enforcement process or acknowledged by the institution, this NLI shall be declared null and void. Such declaration shall not take place until all appeals to the NCAA or conference for restoration of eligibility have been concluded.

6.   **Mutual Release Agreement.** A release procedure shall be provided in the event the institution and I mutually agree to release each other from any obligations to the NLI. If I receive a formal release, I shall not be eligible for competition at a second institution during my first academic year of residence there and shall lose one season of competition. The form must be approved by me, my parent or legal guardian, and the Director of Athletics of the institution named on page 1. A copy of the release form shall be filed with the conference which processes this NLI.

a.   **Authority to Release.** A coach is not authorized to void, cancel or give a release to this NLI.

b.   **Extent of Release.** A release from this NLI shall apply to all participating institutions and shall not be conditional or selective by institution.

7.   **Only One Valid NLI Permitted.** I understand that I may sign only one valid NLI, except as listed below.

a.   **Subsequent Signing Year.** If this NLI is rendered null and void under Item 5, I remain free to enroll in any institution of my choice where I am admissible and shall be permitted to sign another NLI in a subsequent signing year.

b.   **Junior College Exception.** If I signed a NLI while in high school or during my first year in junior college, I may sign another NLI in the signing year in which I am scheduled to graduate from junior college. If I graduate, the second NLI shall be binding on me; otherwise, the original NLI I signed shall remain valid.

8.   **Recruiting Ban After Signing.** I understand that all participating conferences and institutions are obligated to respect my signing and shall cease to recruit me upon my signing this NLI. I shall notify any recruiter who contacts me that I have signed.

9.   **Institutional Signatures Required Prior to Submission.** This NLI must be signed and dated by the Director of Athletics or his/her authorized representative before submission to me and my parents (or legal guardian) for our signatures. This NLI may be mailed prior to the initial signing date. When a NLI is issued prior to the initial signing date, the "date of issuance" shall be considered to be the initial signing date and not the date that the NLI was signed or mailed by the institution.

3

10. **Parent/Guardian Signature Required.** My parent or legal guardian is required to sign this NLI regardless of my age or marital status. If I do not have a living parent or a legal guardian, this NLI may be signed by the person who is acting in the capacity of a guardian. An explanation of the circumstances shall accompany this NLI.

11. **Falsification of NLI.** If I falsify any part of this NLI, or if I have knowledge that my parent or guardian falsified any part of this NLI, I understand that I shall forfeit the first two years of my eligibility at any NLI participating institution as outlined in Item 2.

12. **14-Day Signing Deadline.** If my parent or legal guardian and I fail to sign this NLI within **14 days** after it has been issued to me, it will be invalid. In that event, another NLI may be issued within the appropriate signing period.

13. **Institutional Filing Deadline.** This NLI must be filed with the appropriate conference by the institution named on page 1 within **21 days** after the date of final signature or it will be invalid. In that event, another NLI may be issued within the appropriate signing period.

14. **No Additions or Deletions Allowed to NLI.** No additions or deletions may be made to this NLI or the Mutual Release Agreement.

15. **Appeal Process.** I understand that the NLI Steering Committee has been authorized to issue interpretations, settle disputes and consider petitions for release from the provisions of this NLI where there are extenuating circumstances. I further understand its decision may be appealed to the Collegiate Commissioners Association, whose decision shall be final and binding.

16. **Official Time for Validity.** This NLI shall be considered to be officially signed on the final date of signature by myself or my parent (or guardian). If no time of day is listed, an 11:59 p.m. time is presumed.

17. **Statute of Limitations.** This NLI shall carry a four-year statute of limitations.

18. **Nullification of Other Agreements.** My signature on this NLI nullifies any agreements, oral or otherwise, which would release me from the conditions stated on this NLI.

19. **If Coach Leaves.** I understand that I have signed this NLI with the institution and not for a particular sport or individual. For example, if the coach leaves the institution or the sports program, I remain bound by the provisions of this NLI.

I certify that I have read all terms and conditions in this document, and fully understand, accept and agree to be bound by them. *(All three copies of this NLI must be signed individually.)*

SIGNED_____   _____   _____
                          Prospect   Date   Time
                                                                            (Day/Month/Year)   (A.M./P.M.)

_____
            Prospect's Social Security Number

SIGNED_____   _____   _____
              Parent or Legal Guardian   Date   Time
                                                                            (Day/Month/Year)   (A.M./P.M.)

4

statute of limitation. The four year time limit can conflict with state law, but it has not been challenged very often. The NLI has a provision that nullifies all agreements oral or otherwise that would release a signee from the NLI conditions. In other words, you just cannot change this thing!

Just above the signature line is the final clause in the NLI. This clause is set apart and highlighted in a distinct box. This is the Coach Leaving Clause and plainly indicates that the recruit is signing *with the school and NOT with the coach.* That can become a sticking point in the lives of recruits because of the recruiting rapport developed between athlete and recruiter. If the coach leaves the school, the player remains strictly bound by the NLI.

The NLI is signed by the recruit, his parents and/or guardian and the NLI is dated and timed. On the first page, the NLI is issued by the athletic director at the particular school and signed by that A.D. Once signed in triplicate, the athlete is on his way to whatever awaits him at his or her new institution of higher learning.

Does it all look and sound fascinating? Your author was frankly surprised at the complex nature of this contract.

Signing the NLI is no simple matter these days. The NLI has gone from the one page simplicity to the four page contractual monstrosity. It is, however, structured in simple terms and bold letters.

As you gaze on this coveted Recruiting Holy Grail, just consider that some of the student-athletes that sign the NLI have trouble merely reading and writing. Just imagine the "intellectually challenged" athlete sitting down and viewing the NLI for the first time!

CHAPTER 7

Recruiting Glossary

CASUAL OR NOT-so-casual readers of this book may
detect a cynical note about the goings-on in collegiate recruiting. There is a huge reason for this—your author literally
backed into this business of following high school and JUCO players
and their quests for higher education.

For years, I never gave a flying flip about recruiting. The whole
process seemed like the ugly underbelly of a giant monster. You knew
it was there, you just didn't want to see it. My years of legal training
told me that you had to be skeptical and not delve into rumor, speculation, and hearsay. But rumor, speculation, and hearsay are the very
backbone of recruiting. This flaunting of truths and half-truths is just
what people crave and all real recruiting buffs can draw the line.
Well......maybe.

It all seemed so senseless and a waste of time. After all, how much
impact can *one* recruit make? It was explained to me in no uncertain
terms that recruiting is the *lifeblood of every college athletic program*.
Without competitive players, how can you field a competitive program? When you put it in those terms, you can easily see the importance to fans, coaches, and the schools.

As I mentioned, I backed into this profession of writing and reporting about recruiting. Now, I look into the subject for 35 out of 52
weeks and then some for the *Ole Miss Spirit*. Just how I backed into
the media business is a story that I retell for civic groups, interviews,
and curious folk. I won't waste your time on that story in this book,
but I do want to share some of the silliness encountered when looking
at recruiting.

This chapter is devoted to education, enlightenment, and entertainment. Over the last decade or so, a whole new language has emerged

out of the recruiting boom. In many ways, this new language is as complicated as Klingonese from the *Star Trek* sagas, but this world of "signingspeak" can also be as simple as scoring a two on the ACT.

This chapter is also dedicated to a friend from Jackson, Mississippi, who suggested this chapter when he heard about this project. He will remain nameless, but he helps compose the poster board at the Signing Day party at Lyles Carpets for the Rebel Club of Jackson, so he is definitely into "the recruiting thing." Although he will deny it if you ask him anywhere on the street or in private, my friend and I share a subscription to the *Wrestling Observer* newsletter put out by Dave Meltzer in Campbell, California. This newsletter, which keeps us thoroughly in laughter over the course of a year, is devoted to reporting the "truth" about professional wrestling, which is why my friend will seek to have my head on a platter once this book is published. Anyway, with credits and apologies to my pal, here is an enjoyable glossary of recruiting terms in no particular order:

Heard anything?—The buzzwords used over the phone or in person when someone wants to find out the latest recruiting information. This phrase instantly keys in the recruiting buff and lets him know that someone needs some fresh scoop.

letter-of-intent—The document approved by the NCAA, college, and conference, if applicable, that binds a student-athlete to receive an athletic scholarship from a particular college or university. The document must be signed by the player, his parent or guardian, and a representative of the school. The player must meet all requirements outlined by the NCAA before he can actually receive the scholarship documents. This is also the document that is the object of desire on Signing Day and is subject to the NCAA "Fax and FedEx" Rule. (See Chapter 6, National Letter of Intent).

Signing Day—The day the NCAA designates as the start of the time period when high school and junior/community college players can sign letters-of-intent. The days vary depending upon the sport, but football signing day is normally the first Wednesday in February, and basketball, baseball, and all other spring sports have Signing Day in April. (See Chapter 4, Signing Day.)

early signing period—A week set aside in November by the NCAA where basketball, baseball and other sports can sign high school and junior/community college players to letters-of-intent.

JUCO—Shortened nickname for players who are attending a junior college or community college. Alternative nicknames include "JC's" and "CC's."

blue chipper—A top-notch player who can probably enter an athletic program and become an instant contributor or star.

stud duck—A blue chipper who can play instantly for any program in the country. Alternate terms include *hoss, stud, beast,* and anything else that suits your fancy.

manimal—A blue chipper who is a huge football player or tall and powerful basketball player. Phrase frequently used about defensive linemen and linebackers in football and power forwards and centers in hoops.

prospect—Any high school, prep, or JUCO player who is athletically talented and seeking to enter a college or university to play a specific sport by way of a college scholarship.

suspect—Any high school, prep, or JUCO player who is borderline on athletic ability and is seeking to enter a college or university to play a specific sport by way of a college scholarship.

impact player—Any player who can step in as a JUCO or a high school player and contribute immediately to an athletic program by starting or playing in his first season.

Prop 48—Player who is athletically talented but lacks the NCAA requirements of a 2.00 grade-point average in core curriculum courses or the required ACT or SAT scores. If the player lacks the test scores, he or she can enter school on a college scholarship, but then must sit out one full year to achieve in the classroom. Such players will lose one year of eligiblity. Instead of the usual five years to get four years of eligibility, they will have only three years of eligibility. (Although they may have some years restored by the NCAA.) Usually, Prop 48 players enter a junior or community college or merely sit out a year. Many pay their own way to the school that signs them, but that is very rare.

core—The nickname for the NCAA requirement of a 2.00 grade-point average (GPA) needed for a student athlete to be eligible for a collegiate athletic scholarship. The "core" grade must be in subjects such as math, social sciences, history, English, etc., which are essential or "core" to a high school graduate having basic educational skills.

score—The nickname for the NCAA requirement of a 17 on the ACT test or 700 on the SAT college entrance tests needed for a student athlete to be eligible for a collegiate athletic scholarship. It is good advice for potential recruits to take the ACT or SAT in their junior year so they can easily be recruited and be considered a prime prospect in their senior years.

highly recruited—A player who receives literature and offers from many top-ranked colleges and universities to sign letters-of-intent with their school.

"Can't Miss"—See *blue chipper* and *highly recruited*. It's a combination of both.

transfer student—A student who transfers from one school to another. Under current NCAA rules, a student can transfer after receiving permission from the school he is attending and obtaining a release from his scholarship. That student must sit out a year before entering competition for the new school.

Placed—When a college program assists or helps a student-athlete out of high school enter a JUCO program because of lack of eligibility for whatever reason. It is very common, in football and somewhat common in basketball for coaches to "place" these players at a certain JUCO that is close to home so they can be easily recruited back into their programs once their JUCO academic record is sound enough for a transfer.

"The List"—A list of names of high school, prep, or JUCO players and where they may sign. Lists vary from person to person; they may be listed by position, name, alphabetical, school, and many are computerized. Information a list can contains depends on who compiles the list, but most recruiting followers will include the name, hometown, school they are attending, height, weight, speed in the 40-yard dash, and if the player is academically eligible.

"Mr. Whatever"/All-State—The title an outstanding high school, prep, or JUCO player receives for outstanding athletic achievement. Such an award or designation supposedly increases the player's chances of signing a college letter-of-intent and is supposedly a measuring stick or evaluation of the player's worth on recruiting lists.

commitment—The verbal promise of a player to sign a letter-of-intent with a certain college or university. Most players announce to the media that they are "committed" to sign a letter-of-intent with a certain school just before Signing Day. Commitments, however, are not legally binding and it is common for players to change their minds, break their "commitments," and sign with another program at the last minute. A "private" commitment means that a player has not publicly announced his intentions to attend a certain school but has privately assured the school's coaches that he will sign with that school. A "public" commitment means that a player has made an announcment in public, usually to the media, that the player will sign with a certain school.

recruiting "guru"—The nickname for publishers, founders, writers, broadcasters and/or other persons who follow the recruiting process and players religiously and who offer specialized recruiting lists, 900 numbers, magazines, and newsletters to the public at large. (These are not the same gurus you find high on mountaintops in the Himalayas! These are just guys with extremely outrageous long distance phone bills, handy computers, fax machines, and a publisher.) A "guru" makes his living off his recruiting service almost exclusively.

contact period—Time period designated by the NCAA when authorized and certified athletic department staff members can make in-person, off-campus recruiting contacts and evaluations of high. school, prep, and JUCO players. An exception is made for service academies who recruit under different guidelines for military service aspects. For football, teams can only make contact after July 1 of the prospect's junior year. Off-campus recruiters must be certified by NCAA rules, which is designed to allow only the coaches who know the rules to go out on the road. The head coach is now allowed only *one* in-home visit and he must take an assistant coach with him—usually the position coach of the player involved or the assistant that has been actively recruiting the player. In football, the contact periods are the months of December and January until Signing Day in February. Contact period in January and February is broken up by the American Football Coaches Association Convention, the NCAA Convention and by the 48-hours, before and 72 hours after Signing Day. This is the time period in which recruits can officially visit campus. A recruit is allowed five official visits to campus and these official visits are defined as those visits paid by the school or by a representative of the school's athletic interests.

evaluation period—A time period as designated by the NCAA when coaches visit the high school coaches and JUCO coaches and watch film, live games, or practice to determine in person how good a recruit really is. This is where authorized staff members of the athletic department assess the academic qualifications and playing ability of prospects. During this period, there can be no in-person off-campus contacts with that prospect. The coaches can only watch games, practices, films, or tapes of the player. If there is "incidental contact" with a recruit, the coach can exhibit "normal civility" (See *incidental contact* and *normal civility*.) The month of May and the weekdays in October and November are the evaluation periods for football. Basketball evaluation periods occur on different levels.

quiet period—A time period designated by the NCAA when in-person contacts with a recruit can be made on campus only. No in-person off-campus contacts or evaluations may be made in this time period. This is also referred to as the "unofficial visit," where prospects visit campus on their own and at their own expense to watch a game, etc. Prospects are allowed to receive a complimentary ticket to the game and that is all a school is allowed to give—no entertainment allowed. Contact can only happen here if the recruit initiates the contact at his own expense.

dead period—A time period designated by the NCAA where there can be no inperson contacts or evaluations on or off campus with a recruit. During a dead period, no official or unofficial visits are allowed in any form or fashion and no coaching staff member can serve as a speaker or attend any meeting or banquet where any prospects may be in attendance. No coaching staff member can visit the prospect's school in any way. Staff members, however, can still write or telephone prospects. Only one phone call a week to a recruit is allowed under NCAA rules.

legacies—A recruit or recruits who have a relative or parent/guardian that played a sport or attended a certain school. If that school is successful in signing the recruit, then that recruit becomes a "legacy signing." The school where the relative attended is considered to have the edge and upper hand in signing the player who is a legacy.

theory of relativity—See *legacies*. Same thing, different name. If one player signs with one school, odds are that the player's brother, sister, cousin, nephew, etc. will sign with the same school provided they can play. It is difficult for teams to turn down legacies simply because it promotes some bad "family blood" and is a mark of betrayal to a school's tradition and loyalty of alumni and fans.

package deal—A situation that involves two or more recruits with common interests towards one school. This is a "Three Musketeer" recruiting development. If one recruit has a relative, usually a brother or sister, that goes to one school, chances are the younger brother or sister will follow that brother, sister, or other relative to the same school. This arrangement also happens when a group of teammates who are all eligible and can play decide to stay together and attend the same school.

sweetheart deal—Almost the same as a package deal, but it is also called the "Godfather Deal" where a recruit is made an offer he "can't refuse." These involve position promises. Example: "If you sign with us, we guarantee we'll let you play quarterback." New trend in this area is allowing a football recruit to play baseball in the same vein as Bo Jackson at Auburn and "Neon" Deion Sanders at Florida State.

kidnapping—The illegal practice of hiding out prospects from coaches of rival schools just before Signing Day. The Dead Period is used to eliminate this practice, but it is frequently broken. Most common kidnapping excuse: "He's out on a squirrel hunting trip!" No, this is not the same type of kidnapping that can send you to the slammer!

inking—The act of a recruit signing a letter-of-intent.

incidental contact—Occurs when a coach accidentally bumps into a prospect that coach is recruiting on an evaluation trip to the player's school or game or on any other social occasion.

normal civility—What a coach can say to a recruit during an "incidental contact." Since the coach cannot speak to the player about signing with that school and since it would be socially incorrect for the coach not to say anything, the coach can usually go "Hi! How are you?" and let it go at that. ("How'z yur momma 'n' 'em?" is a frequent Mississippi greeting!)

official visit—The time period where a recruit can visit the campus of a school he is interested in signing with free of charge. The school or a representative of the school can pay the recruit's way for the whole weekend and provide entertainment. Recruits must have taken the ACT or SAT tests before going on official visits under NCAA rules. The NCAA limits a school to a total of 70 official paid visits per recruiting period.

unofficial visit—The time period, usually during a school's regular athletic season, where a recruit can go to the campus on his own and at his own expense. The school can provide the recruit a complimentary ticket to the team's game, but cannot provide any entertainment of any type whatsoever.

visit—Usually refers to an official visit. Whenever a player "gives a visit" to a school, that means the player will be on campus for a weekend official visit.

Fax and FedEx Rule—The NCAA rule that states that a player can no longer sign his or her letter-of-intent with a coach of that school witnessing the signing. The player must now sign the letter-of-intent with his or her parent or guardian and send that letter-of-intent back to the school by regular or express mail. The player can fax the letter-of-intent back to the school, but the rule specifically states that the player is not officially bound to the school until the original signed letter-of-intent arrives at the school by regular or express mail.

representative of university's athletic interests—Anyone who, under the definitions of the NCAA, is a school representative. The definition is extremely vague and overbroad and could include your average garden-variety card-carrying season-ticket-buying fan or alumnus. The NCAA uses this broad definition to prevent alumni or fan "bag men" from delivering cash and other prizes to recruits illegally to entice the player to sign with a certain school. By definition, mere neighbors to a prospect could be considered to be a "representative of a university's athletic interests." Such a "representative" does not have to be connected with a school in any official or unofficial capacity. They only have to be a fan of that school.

recruiting nut—Person who follows the progress of recruiting in any sport on a large or grand scale. This person usually calls the 900 numbers plus the call-in shows and has multiple-subscriptions to recruiting services. Most recruiting nuts compile their own recruiting lists. Also known as "recruitnik" or recruiting fanatic.

summer camps—Camps conducted by schools geared at bringing 13- to 15-year olds on campus and providing them instructions in various sports. The coaches participate in these with an eye towards building rapport with future talent and increasing their recruiting base. Coaches also receive much, if not all, of the income from these camps as an income supplement.

extra benefits rule—NCAA rules that prohibit student-athletes from receiving "perks" or "extras" that other college students do not have access to. Examples include free "loans" or cash payments, cars, extra-special summer jobs, free iclothing, free food other than what is offered at the school under scholarship, and any other "freebie" that may be interpreted as being an "extra benefit" to a player.

redshirt—The act of holding a player out of competition for one year. Players usually have five years to complete four years of eligibility. A redshirted player cannot compete in regular competition, but can practice with his or her team. Prop 48 players, however, fall into a different category and can only attend school and cannot practice with a team. Players are frequently redshirted when they enter college, particularly in football, unless they are impact players and can earn them selves spots on the roster during preseason practice of their freshman year. Hardship redshirts are granted when players are injured in the early part of the athletic season or for academic reasons. The NCAA grants the hardship redshirts routinely upon application by the school on behalf of the athlete. Decisions on redshirts can be made throughout the course of an athletic season; however, once a player enters competition, he is considered as participating and the potential redshirt year is gone.

filled our needs—Coachspeak heard nearly every signing day. Whether they consider their recruiting classes good or bad, coaches usually, at some time or another, say they have "filled their needs" with the players they have signed.

CHAPTER 8
Slippin' Through the Cracks

EVERY YEAR thousands of young men and women who are athletically talented don't receive college scholarships. Most are academically qualified and raring to go, but the NCAA scholarship restrictions have made recruiting a strict numbers game. Many good players miss out on that numbers game and have to look elsewhere in smaller divisions at smaller schools to receive a free ticket to a higher education. In recruiting street language, these kids "slip through the cracks."

Some of them will land scholarships and some of them will go on to stardom at the schools and in the pro ranks. A very good Mississippi example is running back Fred McAfee, who played at Mississippi College, the Division II school located at Clinton. Fred is an extremely versatile running back who can do it all—run, catch, pass, block. He helped lead his Choctaws to the 1989 Division II National Championship and MC almost claimed that honor in 1990, falling just short in the semifinals. (As discussed previously, the national title was later forfeited due to NCAA penalties.) Fred was named to the Mississippi College Hall of Fame, a testament to his academic excellence, popularity, and wonderful personality and attitude.

Fred was drafted in the late rounds of the NFL draft by the New Orleans Saints. It looked as if he would stay on the reserve or taxi squad all year in 1991, but injuries in the Saints' running backs ranks moved Fred up the depth chart. Saints head coach Jim Mora started working Fred into the offense gradually in mid-season. Near the end of the year, McAfee was the Saints' leading rusher and a fan favorite.

When Fred was being recruited out of Philadelphia, Mississippi, the "Big Three" schools and most of the SEC teams completely ignored him. This is a fine example of "slippin' through the cracks." Fred was good enough for Division II 1989 National Champion MC and the 1991 Western Division Champion New Orleans Saints, but he was not good enough for Ole Miss, State, or Southern.

The Fred McAfee story is a good one to learn for those schools who take a chance on the lesser known prep prospects. There are more athletic scholarships available than the average fan thinks. For example, in NCAA football, there are 437 total scholarships for the taking each year. Division IA has 107 schools, Division II has 120 schools and Division III has 212 schools. The NAIA has 164 schools that play football. Division IAA features 86 total programs. Those are a lot of schools for athletes to look over each year.

The basketball numbers are much higher. There are a total of 798 NCAA basketball teams in the NCAA. Of that number, 296 play ball in Division I, 206 are in Division II, and 296 schools are in Division III. The NAIA features 430 hoops teams.

In recent years, some very well-meaning services have grown up around players who "slip through the cracks." These services are geared towards linking the under-recruited player to one of those scholarships listed above. Currently, there are five companies nationwide that cater to the athletes and their families in their quest for an athletic scholarship. Considering that the average college education and scholarship could range anywhere from $25,000 to $50,000, depending on the university, then you can see that this is a lucrative business.

It's also a risky one. Many of these services are geared towards notifying coaches of the players available out there. Many of these services have success stories to back them up. For every successful placement, however, there is probably an unsuccessful placement and a bitter set of parents and players. The following list of recruiting placement services is not endorsed or guaranteed by the writer, rather, this merely tells what the services do for their clients. This list is intended to inform and outline who and what these services are and how they could help a high school or JUCO player hook on with a school and receive a scholarship. If one player is placed at a college and university as a result of someone finding out about the services in this book, then the purpose of the list has been accomplished. Most of these services provide a money-back guarantee within a specified time period, but, it should be noted and emphasized that *no service* can guarantee that an athlete will receive an athletic scholarship. This list is alphabetical and includes information provided by survey sheets forwarded to each service. An editorial comment by the author is included at the end of each profile and these comments are based on neutral observations and conversations with subscribers and other parties with recruiting backgrounds.

*****

COLLEGE PROSPECTS OF AMERICA (CPOA)

Address: 1221 W. Hunter Street, Logan, Ohio 43138
New address as of Jan. 1, 1992: 12682 College Prospects Drive, Logan, Ohio 43138, or P. 0. Box 269, Logan, Ohio 43138

Phone & Fax numbers: (614) 385-6624, (614) 385-9065 fax

Publications: *The Prospector*, a monthly newsletter for company and athletic emphasis news and *The Gold Mind*, a monthly newsletter on academic emphasis news. Newsletters are distributed to franchisees and company representatives only.

Ratings System: Prep and high school coaches are asked to rate their athletes on their ability to play at the various college levels. In addition, directors of the company compile the athletes' times, statistics, and other vital information and match them to college levels reported to the company by college coaches. The company then sends profiles of the athlete to all colleges and universities where there is a good match both on the athletics and also the academic background and test scores. The service charges $445 for nationwide mailing of one-page profile to an average of 500 to 600 colleges. A smaller $389 fee is available for regional mailing only. Updates are sent after the athlete's senior season, but the service targets sophomores and juniors.

Background: Originator of service is Keith Fox, who helped put himself through college by owning and operating a bait shop and boat livery for years in Conneaut, Ohio. Keith's sales and business background developed at the age of 14. He received a B.S. degree in marketing at Bowling Green State University and was employed out of college at Dow Corning Corporation of Midland, Michigan, as a technical sales representative. As a result of his employment, Keith had a territory of 13 states in the southwestern and southeastern United States. After three years at Dow, Keith then became an independent sales representative with a direct sales company. Over the next five years, Keith became vice president in charge of sales for the United

93

Kingdom and then became vice president of sales for the Caribbean, northern South America and Central America. In 1971 Keith left direct sales and opened a 500-acre hunting resort in southeastern Ohio. This facility is a popular resort with accommodations for up to 50 guests and visitors from Saudi Arabia, Egypt, Japan, Canada and all over the U.S. In 1986, Keith leased out his resort and created College Prospects of America. Currently CPOA operates 200 franchises in the U.S., Canada, Mexico and the United Kingdom. Keith Fox was Small Businessman of the Year for his efforts in his county and was a finalist for *Inc.* magazine's Entrepreneur of the Year Award for Central Ohio. He is a member of the Logan-Hocking Chamber of Commerce Board of Directors and a member of the Hocking County Tourism Board of Directors. Franchises in CPOA cost between $5,000 and $60,000 depending upon student enrollments in the area of the potential franchise.

Comments: CPOA is one of the better recognized services in the business. The company functions through representatives scattered throughout the U.S. and the company will provide a list of representatives in each state. The service has on file endorsement letters from the recruiting coordinators or coaches of Indiana University in football, the University of Alabama in track, Tennessee Tech in volleyball ,and Utah State in football.

*****

COLLEGIATE ATHLETIC NETWORK (CAN)

Address: 6300 N.W. 5th Way, Fort Lauderdale, Florida 33309

Phone & Fax number: (305) 772-9155, (305) 772-0798 fax
Special 800 number for parents: 1-800-344-4777

Publications: Information book entitled *Making the Right Decisions* detailing the application process for colleges and hints on improving chances for receiving sports scholarship plus NCAA rules and recruiting schedules. Service provides resume, sample letters to use for writing to college coaches, and a listing of name and statistics on database.

Ratings System: The service generates personalized computer reports from database of over 2,000 colleges offering over $300 million in sports scholarships and grants according to brochure entitled "Wanna' Play In College?" To use the services, you send in $49.95

94

plus $4.95 for shipping and handling (total of $54.90). Florida residents must pay additional $3.00 state tax. Credit cards are accepted. There is a money-back guarantee for 30 days and all a person has to do is send the materials back to the service with no questions asked. The athlete's information, statistics ,and other background are placed into a database that is available for free to college coaches. Coaches search the database for their needs and pick athletes from this information. Service claims to have spoken with more than 12,000 head coaches in every college sport and the service also claims that there is data on over 200,000 sports positions available across the U.S. Brochure allows athlete to pick sport and provides information as to additional "personal collegiate counseling service." The athlete will receive a list of 10 to 15 colleges that will fit his or her profile along with the names of the coaches and sample letters. A videotape is available through high school coaches or the service will provide the tape introducing the service.

Background: The Collegiate Athletic Network is a wholly owned subsidiary of Sports Tech International, Inc., which is the company that designs computerized video editing and analysis systems used by the NFL, NBA, NHL, and Major League Baseball plus hundreds of NCAA and high school teams in all kinds of sports. AT&T is listed as the official sponsor of the CAN and the brochure is apparently a slick publication of AT&T. The CAN has a Board of Advisors with the following NCAA coaches and officials listed: Bobby Bowden, Head football coach at Florida State University; Rick Pitino, head basketball coach at the University of Kentucky; Pat Summitt, head women's basketball coach at the University of Tennessee; Eliot Teltscher, tennis coach at Pepperdine University; Sigi Schmid, soccer coach at UCLA; Sam Bell, track and field coach at Indiana University; Dr. James Frank, commissioner of the Southwestern Athletic Conference; and Ken Purcell, athletic director and head football coach at Allen High School, Allen, Texas.

Comments: The service boasts an impressive list of coaches on its Board of Advisors. Service is computer oriented and depends on usage of database by college coaches. This is one of the least expensive services on the market.

*****

NATIONAL COACHES COUNCIL (NCC)

Address: 1348 East 3300 South, Salt Lake City, Utah 84152-0190
P. O. Box 520190, Salt Lake City, Utah 84152-0190

Phone & Fax number: (801) 484-4100, (801) 484-5856 fax
Special 800 number: 1-800-726-1213

Publications: Brochure entitled *The Name of the Gain* available to interested athletes.

Ratings System: The NCC gathers information on registered athletes including athletic and academic background. The data is then verified by the athlete and his or her parent and/or guardian. The coach of the athlete completes an evaluation form. A "College Search Fact Finder" is provided which helps the athlete select a list of 15 colleges. A "power rating" is assigned to the athlete which shows how the athlete compares with other athletes nationally and assists the athlete in finding the right market or correct level of athletic competition (Division IA, IAA, II, III, NAIA, etc.). The college coach is sent a four- page profile and the athlete can add additional colleges for an additional fee. The initial cost is $295 for the profile and 15 target college mailouts. The $295 fee can be paid in $95 payments with signing of "CDM" note received by NCC Home office. Additional colleges cost $7 per college. Within 24 hours of initial payment, the athlete receives a welcome letter, a General Athlete Profile work sheet, a Sport Specific Profile work sheet, a Coach's Evaluation work sheet, a Goals work sheet, a College Screening "Fact Finder," a Final Check-list, and a return envelope. The profile work sheets and fact finders are sent to the home office. Within 72 hours of receipt of those items, NCC then sends out a letter with instructions for corrections plus power ratings and lists of colleges, a Proof of Profile, a Listing of Colleges that sponsor the athlete's particular sport, a listing of colleges that meet the Fact Finder criteria, a forum for selecting colleges, and a return envelope. Within 48 hours of receiving the final corrections and 15 college selections, the NCC then sends a confirmation letter that profiles have been sent to the 15 colleges and instructions to the athlete about contacting the college within 30 days if the college does not respond to the NCC response cards sent. A corrected profile and the NCC evaluation wrap-up sheet for parents is also sent to the athlete. It is at this point that the NCC sends out an introductory letter, a profile, two response cards for the athlete and the NCC, and a request for info about the program. A representative of the NCC follows up on all of this at each stage and is responsible for reporting back to the home office on the athlete's progress and for follow-up on college responses. The NCC describes all of this as a "closed circle" process. If the athlete is a multisport athlete, there are additional charges. There is the $295. charge for the primary sport, $125. for the second sport and $125. for the third sport. Credit card service available. The NCC has a 30-day money-back guarantee. If the athlete is not satisfied, the NCC registration can be cancelled at any time within the 30-day period after the initial registration date and a full refund will be provided.

Background: Burke Maxfield is the primary contact person for the home office in Salt Lake City, Utah. According to information provided in the service survey, the National Coaches Advisory Council was designed by the following list of coaches who have collectively won over 50 national championships: Tom Osborne, head football coach of University of Nebraska; Don James, head football coach of the University of Washington; Lavell Edwards, head football coach of Brigham Young University; Lute Olson, head basketball coach of the University of Arizona; Billy Tubbs, head basketball coach of the University of Oklahoma; Pat Henry, head coach for men's and women's track at LSU; Gene Stephenson, head baseball coach of Wichita State University; Jerry Yeagley, head coach of men's soccer of Indiana University; Mick Haley, head coach of women's volleyball of the University of Texas; Sharron Backus, head coach of women's softball of UCLA; Eddie Rease, head coach of men's swimming and diving of the University of Texas; Dick Gould, head coach of men's tennis of Stanford University; Richard Quick, head coach of women's Swimming and diving of Stanford University; Joe Seay, head coach of wrestling of Oklahoma State University; Gregg Grost, head coach of men's golf of the University of Oklahoma; and Al Scates, head coach of men's volleyball of UCLA.

Comments: The NCC has detailed brochures and a complete listing of services provided. The process for the athlete is spelled out in a step-by-step process. The service is extremely specific on what it has to offer the athlete.

*****

NATIONAL COLLEGE RECRUITING ASSOCIATION (NCRA)

Address: 22565 Ventura Blvd., Woodland Hills, California 91364

Phone & Fax number: (818) 225-7500 (818) 225-7537 fax

Special 800 number: 1-800-473-NCRA or 1-800-473-6272

Publications: *Blue Chip Illustrated*, which is a recruiting magazine devoted to listing top athletes in football and basketball. The magazine is published in August, November, December, January, and March plus bonus issues. Cost of the magazine subscription/service is $49.

Ratings System: Athletes are data based by their information and the service sends out one-page profiles to an average of 300 to 400 colleges. Cost of the service is $395 for the nationwide mailing and there are regional offices that service the athlete during the recruiting process. College coaches have free access to the data base. Only qualified athletes can apply, meaning that the athlete must already meet academic requirements of college before utilizing the service. There is an internal computer rating system for the athletes, which assists in the college "match." If the athlete is not satisfied with the service, the NCRA will provide full refunds of all fees paid. The service claims that they have never had to refund any monies back to any athlete that subscribed to the service.

Background: Jeff Duva created the National College Recruiting Association, Inc. in 1982 as a result of his background in college football. Jeff was an All-American quarterback for the University of Hawaii Rainbows and played in the 1979 Hula Bowl. He was an assistant coach for two years at Hawaii before accepting the offensive coordinator position at California State at Northridge. Jeff has extensive knowledge and experience in the recruiting arena according to his response in the survey. His partner in the NCRA is Rick Kimbrel and together they publish *Blue Chip Illustrated*, which is widely regarded as one of the top recruiting publications in the nation. The NCRA is a splinter service offered by Duva and Kimbrel and claims a 75 percent success rate in placing qualified student-athletes with college programs across the nation. According to Jeff, only one-tenth of one percent of top athletes are listed on the recruiting lists, leaving the remaining athletes across the country open to be recruited. *USA Today* is listed as a frequent caller for information on recruits and signings.

Comments: The NCRA services are complemented and supple-

98

mented by the *Blue Chip Illustrated* information network. The claim of 75 percent success ratio of placing athletes and never having given a refund is impressive. The athletes that subscribe must be qualified in order to enter the service and take advantage of the profile mail-out.

*****

SPORTS MARKETING UNLIMITED (SMU)

Address: 18537 Ashland Avenue, Homewood, Illinois, P. O. Box 748, Glenwood, Illinois 60425

Phone & Fax number: (708) 798-5628, no fax number listed

Publications: Newsletter will be produced for free at later date.

Ratings System: According to Larry L. Morford, president of Sports Marketing Unlimited, the service has no rating system. The service believes that information should be sent only to the colleges that the athlete is interested in attending. Mass mail-outs are not provided unless the athlete specifically requests a mail-out. The service receives information about what division of play the athlete can participate in if granted a college scholarship from the athlete's coach, opposing coaches, the athlete, and his or her parents and/or guardians. This is a small midwestern service that provides an athlete with a list of colleges offering scholarships in his or her sport. The athlete picks out the college and a three- or four-page profile is sent to the college coaches involved. The profiles include the athlete's personal data, high school information, college interest, financial aid information, athletic information, awards and/or honors received in high school, camps attended, statistics, goals, comments, evaluation form, results of tests performed, and a copy of high school or JUCO transcript. Newspaper clippings are sent at extra charge. A videotape of the athlete can also be produced with an introduction plus skills displayed by the athlete. The athlete is provided with a copy of the tape, with the original kept at the home office in the event the copies are lost or damaged. The service will produce and create the videotape at the athlete's direction. Profiles are sent by mass mailout or the service provides a list of colleges and the player can pick from the list. A minimum of 25 profiles must be sent out off this list. An initial registration fee of $50 is required. Mass mailings of 225 profiles will cost $380 and the individual mailings to 25 select colleges cost $1.75 each or a total of $43.75. Videotapes are $110 and transfer of videotapes is

$15. Highlight videos are $45 each. A typical "package" for an athlete using this service would be the $50 registration fee, 25 player profiles mailed at $43.75 and a videotape of $110 for a total of $203.75. The service recommends the player profiles first and then the videotape. Credit cards are accepted and the service is involved in fund-raising as well. If the athlete is not satisfied with the videotape produced, then the tape is produced once more with corrections at no charge. The service prides itself on quality, not quantity and not on the mass mail-outs. The service claims a success rate of 92 percent of placing athletes in college programs.

Background: Larry L. Morford is the president of Sports Marketing Unlimited and has been involved in athletics for many years. In 1986, Larry formed a not-for-profit corporation entitled F.A.S.T., Inc., which stands for Female Athletes for Scholarships and Training. Larry was involved with women's softball with the American Softball Association and felt that not enough was being done to help the average-to-good softball athlete from the Chicago and Northwest Indiana areas to receive college scholarships. He began his service by sending player profiles and videotapes to college coaches on behalf of the athletes. He then established a training program for these athletes to refine their skills in preparation of the player profile and videotape. Initially, there was no charge for this service. In May, 1990, Larry was laid off from his regular job due to a company restructuring. He then formed Sports Marketing Unlimited in June, 1990. At age 50, he began to expand his recruiting services and over the years, he has developed F.A.S.T and Sports Marketing Unlimited to include all sports for all athletes. In response to the survey, Larry made the following comments: "Many recruiting services only do mass mail-ings on the athlete and have in most cases very little videotape ser-vices. While we can do mass mailings to college coaches, we normally don't recommend this to prospective athletes. We believe that the athlete should concentrate on the colleges that he/she would like to attend after graduation from high school or junior college. We can do mass mailings if that is what the athlete wants from us. We feel it is a waste of their money as many colleges that might be interested only finds out that the athlete wasn't interested in attending in the first place. This creates a lot of friction between the recruiting services and college coaches. I am happy to report that we only send in most cases to colleges that the athlete is interested in attending. We have the athlete go through a listing offering athletic scholarships in their sport and mark the ones that they want to pursue.....It is our objective to provide the athlete with what they want in a recruiting service at a reasonable price. We also want to help the athlete all the way through the recruiting process and we are available to answer questions or provide consulting to them."

Comments: This service can be described as the "Mom and Pop" recruiting service. It is small, but with a solid personal touch.

*****

Before he was tossed out on his ear unceremoniously at North Carolina State, the late Jim Valvano, whose team captured the 1983 NCAA basketball title over Houston, had a unique style for recruiting top roundball prospects. Jim would usher a new recruit into a completely dark, totally empty campus arena. He would walk that recruit out onto the court.

All of a sudden, a loud roar and laser lights would erupt all around the recruit. The Wolfpack play-by-play announcer would be heard over the public address system and that recruit would be the hero of a last second shot to win the ACC title game or whatever Valvano had concocted. The shot would, naturally, go in, the crowd roared and the laser light show continued to blaring sounds of music and hoop happiness. An easily impressed prospect would certainly marvel at this style of recruiting.

The NCAA banned this type of P. T. Barnum bunko. Jim Valvano was bounced off campus for recruiting violations. After spending a tenure at ESPN, Jim Valvano was diagnosed as having cancer and passed away in April, 1993. Many other programs pulled this recruiting stunt, but Valvano was the master. Despite his courage in facing his disease, Valvano's recruiting tractics used, abused and ignored talented players who only wanted a chance to compete for a scholarship.

This story is to illustrate that recruiting is played up as being glitzy and glamorous. Outstanding players on high school and JUCO campuses who don't get a second look wouldn't have made it on campus for the official visit to see the light show. Hopefully, this chapter has served to assist the average recruit in receiving a scholarship.

There are only 107 division IA schools that play football and only a small percentage of players can be granted scholarships. A smaller percentage of college players make it in the pros. A college scholarship and a degree lasts a whole lot longer than the Valvano light show. If you know of an athlete that needs one of the above mentioned services, help him or her out. You never know who may be slippin' through the cracks.

CHAPTER 9
The Services

SINCE THE EARLY 1980s, recruiting services have been an ongoing phenomenon. Basically, these services are in the business of providing names and speculation to the uninformed as to where high school and JUCO players will go to college and play football or basketball. It's a multimillion-dollar business and reputation is everything. *The Ole Miss Spirit* and your author sent out inquiries and obtained information about every recruiting service known in the nation.

The results of this survey are included here. These services are the ones that are frequently mentioned in the recruiting community. They all feature different services, different prices, and different backgrounds, and cover different areas. The author and this book does not rate, recommend, or endorse any of the services listed here. Editorial comments are provided at the end of each profile to reflect the perception the average recruiting fan or subscriber has of the particular service. This listing is solely for the benefit of the reader, who may or may not know about these services and what they do.

It is recommended to the reader that the service's publications be reviewed *before* purchasing that service. Most of these recruiting "gurus" will offer free samples before entering a subscription. The author highly advises that you check out what the service has to offer in the way of presentation of information and format before spending any money. Be satisfied with what you want out of the information before buying in. It is estimated roughly that if the average recruiting fan attempted to purchase nearly every service offered and on the recruiting market, the fan would be out at least $1,000 or more. Be selective and pick out what you like among the services before sending in your check or credit card number. The time tested phrase of "Buyer

Beware" definitely applies to these ventures. There is also no way that any service can be 100 percent accurate. Recruits have been know to change their minds without telling anyone. That's the nature of the business. You will also find a listing of radio sports call-in shows and specialty publications at the end of this listing. Because of format and personnel changes, these shows and publications are subject to constant change. The shows and publications listed are geared for the southern part of the U.S. and emphasize whether or not the shows discuss recruiting and who the guests may be. This is not a complete listing and you may know of a show or a publication that covers recruiting. If so, there is an address and phone number in the back of this book to help us update and revise this edition.

All recruiting service listings are alphabetical according to the owner/editor/publisher and are as complete as can be and they include additional biographical information and 900 numbers used. But 900 numbers frequently change or may not be activated during certain times of the year. Menus listed for the 900 numbers are complete as of date of publication. An index as to the common name of the service plus the owner/editor/publisher is included with the table of contents.

*****

TOM BARROWS, JR.

Name of Service: *Southeastern Recruiting*
Address: P.O. Box 57347, Atlanta, Georgia 30343
Phone & Fax numbers: (404) 434-0575, (404) 524-7311 fax
Publications: *Southeastern Recruiting* consists of five newsletters published beginning with a preseason Top 300 players issued on September 1 of each year. Three recruiting updates start on January 4 and continue every two weeks leading up to Signing Day. The final newsletter is the Post-Season Evaluation which provides complete listings of all recruiting classes and ratings of recruits for teams in the SEC, selected ACC teams, and southern independents. Service covers the states of Alabama, Florida, Georgia, Mississippi, Louisiana, North Carolina, South Carolina, and Tennessee. Subscription price for newsletter service is $25.
Ratings System: A 5-star (*****) rating is the highest rating the service assigns to a player. Five-star players have All-American type of potential, and in certain instances and depending on the position and

school he is attending, the player has the potential to be a four-year starter. A 4-star + rating (****+) is assigned to a player who looks to be a certain three-year starter and possible All-SEC or All-ACC player. A four-star player should definitely help a program early in his career and is a possible three-year starter. This system goes as low as two stars. The service rarely assigns a player a 2-star rating even if the service does not have enough information on the player because, in most instances, SEC recruiting coordinators know their business and if they think the recruit is good enough to play in the SEC or ACC, then that is considered good enough for the service to be rated.

900 number service: 1-900-786-4400 at $1.49 per minute. The 900 number menu includes state-by-state breakdown of top recruits and visits and the number includes the following states: Louisiana, Mississippi, Alabama, Georgia, Florida, North Carolina, South Carolina, and Tennessee. As official visits begin, the 900 number is updated to include which recruits are visiting which schools each particular weekend.

Background: Tom Barrows, Jr. is the editor of *Southeastern Recruiting*. Tom graduated in 1982 from Florida State with a degree in public relations. He interned in the Media Relations Dept. at FSU and became interested in sports and the role the media played with the various programs. He describes himself as a football fanatic and became interested in college football recruiting which he calls "the lifeblood of a college program." Tom saw a number of top high school players while attending college and he was surprised at how fast they were able to jump into the big time and impact a college team. The first year he followed recruiting, he did it all just for fun. As he followed the visits of top recruits and the closer the date approached Signing Day, the more people he talked to and the better contacts he made. By the second year, he realized that his hobby was important to the average fan and thus he devoted more time and made more con-tacts.

As Tom indicates, in recruiting it is important to find "inside information" and accurate sources for that information. Those sources, according to Tom, can only be obtained through trial and error. After seven years, Tom claims to have one solid contact at every school in the South as well as a good reputation with high school coaches and newspaper reporters throughout the southern U.S. Tom says he really enjoys recruiting and talking to other fanatics and sharing information. He spends 60 hours a week on recruiting in January and February.

Comments: Tom has a well-established service, but it is not a high-profile operation. He is well known in Atlanta and the state of Georgia, but he is not well known nationally. Tom's operation is specialized towards the South.

*****

BILL BUCHALTER

Name of Service: *Bill Buchalter Recruiting Newsletter*
Address: 344 B. Hillcrest Street, Altamonte Springs, Florida 32701 or to Bill Buchalter c/o *The Orlando Sentinel*, P. O. Box 2833, Orlando, Florida 32802-2833

Phone & Fax numbers: (407) 830-5402 (h) or (407) 420-5743 (o), (407) 420-5069 fax at office

Publications: *Bill Buchalter Recruiting Newsletter* is printed six times a year in the months of July, September, November, December, January, and February. The newsletter is released and mailed usually at the end of each of those listed months with the exception of February, with printing set for just after Signing Day. Emphasis is on football, primarily on prospects located in the state of Florida. Subscription to the newsletter costs $25 per year. Bill concentrates on high school and prep players with a dash of JUCO news.

Ratings System: In Bill's own words: "I don't use ratings systems because how can you rate players you don't see!"

900 number: Several as follows: 1-900-884-1100, extension 110 for Florida recruit information, extension 120 covers the SEC, extension 130 covers the ACC, and extension 140 covers national recruiting; 1-900-860-4286 then 4 is the 900 number for *Gator Bait,* a specialty publication for Florida Gator fans and that number deals with recruits for the University of Florida; 1-900-860-4378 then 6 is the 900 number for *Osceola*, a specialty publication for Florida State fans and this number deals with recruits for the Seminoles. All 900 numbers provided by Bill are $1.49 per minute.

Background: Bill Buchalter has been following the recruiting wars in the state of Florida for years. He is the most reliable source for Florida high school and JUCO prospects in terms of information and speculation. Bill is a longtime writer for *The Orlando Sentinel* and he still works daily for his paper. His recruiting activities have been

blossoming for years since the mid-1980s. Bill only recently added his 900 number service and his newsletter is time tested and considered the top info source for the Florida players. With a large number of top prospects in the state of Florida, Bill has all he can handle in figuring out where all of that top talent will sign. Bill's reputation is solid and dependable and he is a super writer. He deals strictly in facts and provides lots of them in his services.

Comments: Bill Buchalter is one of the top recruiting persons in the business. If there's a player in Florida, odds are extremely high that Bill knows all about him and who may sign him. Bill provides information to many other recruiting services and also confirms information for many other "gurus." Bill is the exclusive source for Florida recruits. By concentrating on the state of Florida, Bill is limited in scope, but consider that the Sunshine State produces anywhere from 300 to 400 top players each year. This is an impeccable service and one of the best in the business.

*****

FORREST DAVIS

Name of Service: Forrest Davis' *PrepSports* Recruiting
Address: P. O. Box 94428, Birmingham, Alabama 35220-4428
Phone & Fax numbers: (205) 854-4785 (phone & fax number)
Publications: *PrepSports* recruiting newsletter, which is published monthly from August through April with two issues in January. *PrepSports* is a 12-page newsletter that features high school recruits only on state-by-state basis. Forrest also produces a recruiting annual entitled the *Forrest Davis Southern Football Recruiting Annual* that is on the newsstands in January listing his All American, All-South choices and profiles top players in each of the southern states: Louisiana, Mississippi, Alabama, Georgia, Florida, South Carolina, Kentucky, and Tennessee. Subscription cost for *PrepSports* is $26. for 10 issues, and Forrest will provide a free sample copy if he is called at the above number. Forrest also produces a "Favorite Team" list, which provides a listing of players considering certain schools. This list becomes available on November 1 through the end of January each year. "Favorite Team" lists are computer listings and each list for each team and/or school costs $5.. The "Favorite Team" list is described by Forrest as a method to keep track of players who are really interested in

108

a favorite team. The lists are continuously updated to insure fresh information. This service is only available to *PrepSports* subscribers. Forrest's services concentrate on high school and prep players and do not involve JUCO players in any manner.

Ratings System: Forrest uses a 5-star system. As he describes it, the 5-star rating system has been devised to assign a value to the potential a high school athlete has in relation to his ultimate performance in college. Height, weight, and speed are particularly important in determining the potential any athlete may have according to Forrest. For instance, speed in the 40-yard sprint doesn't show a player's ability to move laterally, to catch a ball, to think quickly, or to run in an elusive fashion. Forrest, therefore, indicates that a wide range of factors must be considered in the evaluation of a prospect. The *PrepSports* system gives a one for the lowest and five for the highest rating. Ratings are assigned based on conversations Forrest personally has with each recruit and/or their coaches and conversations with college coaches. The ratings are as follows:

One Star—a player who may play at sometime in his career, but in all likelihood won't ever start;

Two Star—a player who may start as a senior, but won't contribute greatly until his junior year;

Three Star—a player who may start as a junior and can be expected to contribute as a sophomore;

Four Star—a player who may start as a sophomore and contribute greatly as a freshman and players of this caliber have a good chance at pro ball and college stardom;

Five Star—a player who may start at some time during his freshman year; players on this level are strong bets to play pro ball, be All-Americans and win awards like Heisman Trophies. Forrest says that a player may receive a rating of 6 if he is a 5-Star player and plays quarterback or placekicker, due to the importance of those positions.

After a team has signed all of its recruits, Forrest measures the relative strength by adding together all of the numbers of stars assigned by Forrest to each recruit. He constantly evaluates and updates each rating as necessary. Forrest lives by a strict recruiting golden rule: he never profiles a player without first talking to that player. Every player Forrest rates has been interviewed at some point by Forrest, usually over the phone. He does evaluate some film of recruits, primarily for his local television recruiting updates.

900 number: 1-900-990-7774 at $1.95 for the first minute and .95 cents for each additional minute.

Background: Forrest Davis is another of the pioneers of the recruiting service industry and the first of his kind in the Deep South. The Birmingham, Alabama, native began as a free-lance writer on the subject of football recruiting in 1979. His early articles and columns appeared in several newspapers and sports magazines in the early 1980s. His first full-time column appeared in the now defunct *SEC Sports Journal* which was published by longtime Birmingham writer Ben Cook. While writing for this magazine, Forrest developed his first newsletter format entitled *GoldStar* which first appeared in 1979. Forrest helped to start Max Emfinger in 1979, when he compiled Max's first-ever Dixie South recruits list. Forrest's efforts appeared in Max's original issue of his newsletter and Forrest received the first, and probably only, byline in an Emfinger offering. Forrest still keeps a copy of that first Emfinger newsletter at his home. The success of *GoldStar* grew in the South and Forrest began to appear on numerous radio call-in shows in the area.

In 1984 and 1985, Forrest began to write for Lindy Davis' pre-season football annuals as he compiled the summer SEC preseason recruiting lists. In conjunction with Lindy, Forrest also published his first January annuals, but Lindy's connection with the January maga-zine ended in 1987. In 1988, Forrest created his present format of *PrepSports* and he published his first *Forrest Davis Southern Football Recruiting Annual*, a slick magazine that arrives on the newsstands in January. He started the "Favorite Team List" in 1989.

During the late 1980s, Forrest also started his television appear-ances geared towards football recruiting. From 1986 to 1989, he was a regular at WBMG in Birmingham. He switched stations in 1989 to WBRC. Forrest also has a weekly radio show on WAPI in Birming-ham on Wednesday nights from 7-8 P.M. Forrest recently landed a prestigious show on the SportsSouth cable network, a cable subsidiary of the Turner Broadcasting group. This weekly recruiting program, entitled "Countdown to Signing Day," starts in late November and runs through Signing Day. This may be the most ambitious recruiting show on TV as technical computer advances enable callers to the show to ask for certain player information. A computer then instantly pulls up the player's photo and instant stats on the screen with footage of the player in action. Over 150 top players can be featured on this latest venture into computer technology.

Of all of the recruiting services available, Forrest seems to have conquered the three top media outlets in providing information about high school players in the South: print, radio, and TV. He speaks to well over 500 high school players personally while compiling his information. Consider this fact: Forrest's recruiting efforts are a *part-time job*. He has a full-time job with very gracious and understanding supervisors. Quite an undertaking for a hobby!

Comments: Forrest is one of the most highly respected recruiting followers in the nation, particularly in the South. His specialized style is extremely popular and his information is usually right on the mark. Every player listed or discussed by Forrest has been called directly by Forrest or Forrest has spoken to the player's coach. His ratings system is one of the sounder systems around and very easy to explain. He is a cooperative publisher and well versed in television and radio. Forrest is highly visible and media-ready. Forrest is not without critics, however, as he is frequently accused of concentrating too much on Alabama and he has been criticized from time to time of leaning towards Alabama recruits and not dealing with JUCO players. Those accusations are false and totally groundless and he is solid in contacts with all of the schools in the South. His wide base and extensive contacts with the high school and prep players dispel any knocks, and insure that his service is one of the best. The "Favorite Team" lists are very popular and one of the most frequently asked-for features of his service. Forrest describes this service as "one of the most plagiarized lists in the country." Without a doubt, Forrest is the Head Honcho of Southern Recruiting, and a recruiting pioneer with an outstanding reputation.

*****

JEFF DUVA and RICK KIMBREL

Name of Service: *Blue Chip Illustrated*
Address: 22565 Ventura Blvd., Woodland Hills, California 91364
Phone & Fax numbers: (818) 225-7500, (818) 225-7537 fax
Publications: *Blue Chip Illustrated* is a slick magazine published in August, November, December, January, and March plus bonus

issues. Subscriptions are $59 per year and credit cards are accepted. August issue is a Pre-Season All-American and All-Regional issue; November issue is a Post-Season Wrap-Up for JUCO, high school and prep players; January issue is a Pre-Signing Date issue; December issue features an early official visit report; and March issue is a recruiting re-cap. A fax service named PREP-FAX is available on specific request.

Ratings System: Players are rated based on data from recruiting coordinators and contacts the service has accumulated. The service also has an internal computer ranking system.

900 number: 1-900-RECRUIT or 1-900-7RECRUITat $1.49 a minute. Menu is national variety as *Blue Chip Illustrated* has a national recruiting focus.

Background: Jeff Duva and Rick Kimbrel are the contact persons who originated *Blue Chip Illustrated* and they also operate the National College Recruiting Association. The NCRA services are detailed in a separate profile. Jeff Duva was an All-American quarterback for the University of Hawaii Rainbows and he played in the 1979 Hula Bowl all star game. After graduation, Jeff was an assistant coach at Hawaii before accepting a position as an offensive coordinator at Cal State Northridge. Jeff and Rick created *Blue Chip Illustrated* and the National College Recruiting Association (NCRA) in 1982. Jeff's background is extensive in the area of college recruiting. *Blue Chip Illustrated* recently expanded its services to include basketball recruiting.

Blue Chip Illustrated claims to be the nation's Number 1 college football recruiting service. Information for the service is gathered in May of each year during the normal college coach evaluation periods. The service covers both JUCO and high school players. The service mails out over 3,500 questionnaires to athletes in all 50 states and they receive additional information on over 1,000 of those prospects. The service also breaks down recruiting coverage team by team with a preview of top juniors about to be recruited. The service claims to have released over 1,000 verbal commitments from players prior to Signing Day over the 900 number.

Comments: *Blue Chip Illustrated* is one of two top national recruiting services located in California. (The other being Allen Wallace's *SuperPrep* operation.) Jeff and Rick have a large staff and regional connections due to their NCRA set up. Both services are complemented and supplemented. By expanding to basketball, they hope to tap into a market that follows both sports, something very few recruiting services can claim. They have a slick publication with a bold marketing approach.

*****

MAX EMFINGER

Name of Service: Super Scout Sports, Inc., service entitled *Max Emfinger's National High School Football Recruiting Service* (emblem for service originally consisted of a shield with initials "NHS" similar to the NFL National Football League shield). Recently, the name of his publication was changed to *Max Emfinger's National Blue Chips Magazine*.

Address: 11744 Wilcrest, Suite B115, Houston, Texas 77099

Phone & Fax numbers: (713) 438-2654, (713) 438-FAXX or (713) 438-3299 fax

Publications: Several packages available for subscribers include: national newsletters, four editions, $20; *National Bluechips Recruiting* magazine (includes thousands of high school and JUCO ratings plus photos of All-American and All-Regional teams) $15; Southwest Regional Newsletter (Texas, Oklahoma, Louisiana and Arkansas) three editions, $20; Super Dixie Regional Newsletter (Mississippi, Alabama, Georgia, Florida, Kentucky, South Carolina, and North Carolina) three editions $20; *National Bluechips Recruiting Recap* magazine (final analysis and ratings of Signing Day) $15; Texas Top 400 (top 400 players in Texas) $10; and Super Dixie 400 (top 400 players in Super Dixie states) $10.

Max also offers a faxing service entitled "Super Fax by Max." This fax service sends out recruiting updates on 20 special dates plus a Signing Day bonus fax. Faxes are released by 2:00 A.M. on the specified dates and the total fax package costs $44. Credit cards are accepted for any or all of these packages. Max also requests that the subscriber list his favorite team so that he can tailor the package towards the subscriber.

Ratings System: Max breaks down players into certain categories while focusing on high school and JUCO players. The player positions are quarterback—dropback style, quarterback—run & pass, running back, fullback, wingback, wide receiver, tight end, offensive tackle,

113

offensive guard, offensive center, flanker—big receiver, kicker, punter and athlete.

The "athlete" position allows Max to list players that are super athletes and could play a variety of positions. This also enables Max to list more players in his packages. Max's rating system is on a 4.0 to 6.0 scale with fractional increments, with 6.0 being the highest rating. A 4.0 is a good prospect; a 4.5 is an excellent prospect; a 5.0 is a player with potential for Max's National Top 100 players; a 5.5 rating is for a player that has potential to be on his National Top 100 player with a good senior season; and a 6.0 rating is a player is a potential Max Emfinger National Top 100 with a super senior season, also known as a franchise player. On his lists, if a player is shown in all capital letters, then that player has a known passing test (ACT or SAT) score. If a small circle appears after the player's name, then Max and/or his staff has viewed the player on film or videotape. Only the elite players are placed into the rankings.

900 number: 1-900-454-4551 and costs $1.95 for the first minute and 95 cents for each additional minute and you must be over 18 to call, also known as the "Super Scout Hot Line." Max states that this 900 number is "offering my predictions of where the nation's top prospects will be attending college." The menu of the 900 number is as follows: Press 1 for Notre Dame, Big East Conference teams, Miami; Press 2 for all Southwest Conference teams (SWC); Press 3 for Eastern Division of SEC—Florida, Georgia, Kentucky, South Carolina, Tennessee and Vanderbilt plus Louisville; Press 4 for Western Division of SEC—Alabama, Arkansas, Auburn, LSU, Ole Miss, and Mississippi State plus Tulane; Press 5 for Big 8 Conference teams plus Tulsa; Press 6 for ACC Conference; Press 7 for Big 10 Conference teams including Penn State; Press 8 for Pac 10 Conference teams including Brigham Young University; and Press 9 for Max Emfinger appearances on TV and radio call-in shows. Max promises more lines for the 900 access, less down time, and accessibility for both touchtone and rotary dial phones. Max offers conference calling and interaction with fans on his 900 number enabling recruiting buffs to directly ask Max recruiting questions.

Background: One of the more colorful and original recruiting "gurus" in this cottage industry: Raby Maxwell Emfinger, also known as Max, Emfinger, or "The Super Scout," was a high school running back out of Brownwood, Texas, and he was recruited in 1961 by several major colleges. He signed with Baylor out of high school along with his friend and teammate Lawrence Elkins, who would advance to a pro career with the Houston Oilers. While in college, Emfinger assisted the Baylor coaching staff by sending out letters to other recruits. After two years on the Baylor Bear varsity, Max had an unknown disagreement with Coach John Bridgers in 1963 and he quit the team, received a business degree, and joined the Navy. After his stint with the Navy, Emfinger sold insurance and electronic office equipment. He claims he coached the Carmel High School varsity gridiron team to a district title, but school records dispute this claim and school boosters claim that Max only coached the freshman team at Carmel.

In 1971, Max became a graduate assistant at North Texas State under the guidance of Hayden Fry, but school records do not reveal his being employed in that capacity or in any capacity. In 1973, Max contacted Gil Brandt, who was then the player-personnel director of the Dallas Cowboys. Emfinger had been unsuccessful in his attempts to become a collegiate recruiting coordinator and had sought to land a scout position. Max claims to have been hired by Brandt as a scout, but Brandt indicates that Max was a staff assistant who mainly gathered information or studied film for the Cowboys' staff.

In 1974, Emfinger resigned his low paying-job with the Cowboys and he attempted to enter into a racquetball court enterprise. By 1981, he had to refund membership monies when funding fell through for the racquetball venture and his wife, Ginger, convinced Max to open his own recruiting service companies. Emfinger started with 250 subscribers and had to earn additional money to support his family by umpiring softball games. Now, at age 48, Max boasts anywhere from six to nine recruiting services, 4,000 subscribers, and a very extensive film library. For a fee of $1,000, Max provides personalized scouting and film information to major college programs. He once told *Sports Illustrated* that "what I do is coordinate all recruiting in this country." His computer is adorned with a sign that reads: "My work is so secret even I don't know what I'm doing."

Max has been accused by some college coaches of fudging on numbers and stats and exaggerating here and there. He has also been accused of downgrading the recruiting of schools who do not subscribe to his services. Fans located in the South often criticize Max using the logic that "a guy in Houston, Texas, can't tell you anything about a recruit in Houston, Mississippi." Max has endured negative publicity and vicious personal attacks in recent years.

Nevertheless, Max now claims to have a business that grosses six figures and he is one of the most frequent guests on sports call-in shows across the nation. Emfinger personally visits high school recruits through a spring and summer "Super Scout" tour where he photographs and interviews the top recruits for his yearbooks and recaps. He videotapes top recruits in game action on Fridays and he gathers tapes from other high schools across the nation. The one-of-a-kind entrepreneur remains outspoken and controversial, but recruiting enthusiasts stay loyal to his services and he still cranks out a good chunk of recruiting information each year. Max's staff is composed of editor and general manager John Coppola, radio and TV coordinator Ginger Emfinger, legal consultant Michael Narsete and computer consultant Greg Schulte.

Comments: Without a doubt, Max Emfinger is one of the most controversial and unique figures in recruiting service history. He is also a dauntless promoter who has helped to creat and revolutionized the recruiting industry to a different level over and above "underground newsletters." Max brought recruiting service business into high profile and he maintains a certain "air of affluence" about his services. He is open and candid, but often inconsistent. He offers more services at premium costs than any other service. For that reason alone, recruiting enthusiasts take Max with a grain of salt while tossing money at him for the next newsletter. A high rating of a recruit by Emfinger is considered to have impact with fans, coaches and athletes. The best way to describe his overall reputation in the recruiting world is: Max is Max!

*****

BOB GIBBONS

Name of Service: All Star Sports Publications
Address: P. O. Box 955, Lenoir, North Carolina 28645
Phone & Fax numbers: (704) 758-5827, (704) 758-2270 fax
Publications: *Bob Gibbons' All Star Sports Report* is a newsletter format published 15 times annually. Bob also publishes special

116

basketball reports as follows:

(1) Top 500 High School Senior Basketball Players, which is a pre-season listing of the nation's top players ranked numerically, with Star Sketches on top 50 and photographs; available in late October of each year and priced at $15;

(2) Mid-Year Recruiting Update with a progress report of the top 90 college teams and the current schools are listed for top prep players. Premiere college freshmen are also profiled; available in late March, this report costs $6.50;

(3) Recruiting Wrap-up is a "where they went" report listing the Top 750 seniors and their college choice plus the top 20 recruiting classes, Top JUCO signees and this wrap-up is available in mid June at a price of $6.50;

(4) Juniors Report outlines the Top 500 high school juniors who will be "Prime Prospects" plus numerical rankings and a list of the top sophomores also available in mid-June and priced at $5;

(5) R.A.P. report, which is the recruiting analysis and prospectus evaluating recruiting and the season's outlook for top 90 college teams and a pre-season ranking of top 50 teams and college All-American selections available in late September at a cost of $6.50 .

The complete Basketball Reports special package, which has all five publications as listed here, is priced at $28. If you order the complete package, which consists of the Basketball Reports and the 15 newsletters, the price will be a total of $50. The newsletter service only is a total of $25. The newsletter is touted by Bob as "the most reliable, complete, timely and accurate national recruiting news from America's most respected high school basketball scout and writer." Bob says that he provides readers with an insightful, informative, "no holds barred" look at "the games behind the game." The newsletters and reports cover basketball recruiting primarily with reports on football, women's basketball, and other collegiate sports.

Ratings System: Bob uses a numerical system.

900 number: 1-900-CAN-HOOP or 1-900-226-4667 at 95 cents per minute and available 24 hours. 900 number provides recruiting updates on basketball players only.

Background: A native of Lenoir, North Carolina, Bob Gibbons grew up in basketball country and played high school basketball at Lenoir High. He worked his way through college at North Carolina by waiting on tables for the Monogram Club where he schmoozed with famous Tarheel basketball stars and coaches such as Dean Smith, Doug Moe, Frank McGuire, and many others. Bob worked in several different fields in Raleigh, North Carolina, Atlanta, Georgia, and Montreal, Ontario, before resettling at home in Lenoir. In 1976, Bob was in the insurance business and began pursuing a hobby that followed basketball recruiting. Bob started slowly and began to offer scouting services to colleges across the nation. As his information paid off, so did his services, and his newsletters sprang off this scouting venture. His national newsletter was created in 1978 as his hobby began to emerge as his professional career.

Bob's national reputation as a basketball recruiting "guru" was insured when, in 1981, he accurately predicted that Michael Jordan was the top high school prospect in the nation over Patrick Ewing. It was at this point that his newsletter and scouting "hobby" became nationally acclaimed and accepted. In 1982, his activities had grown to such a level that he gave up the insurance business and started to operate his recruiting services full time. His scouting service for colleges had reached a point that it gave the newsletters solid credibility. *Sports Illustrated* declared Bob's services to be the No. 1 scouting service in America. In a poll conducted by *The Sporting News* of all of the college basketball coaches, Bob's service was rated as the best in the nation, no questions asked. Bob handles player invitations to the prestigious Nike camps held each summer across the country where young talent is honed and displayed for college coaches and pro scouts. According to Bob, the biggest problem with his service is that he personally tries to do too much and doesn't delegate duties very well, although he has expanded and enhanced his staff in Lenoir.

Comments: Bob Gibbons is the top basketball recruiting service in the nation. Hands down, more publications, newspapers, wire services, reporters, television stations, and networks widely utilize Bob's information and opinions than any other recruiting service in the nation. He has a near monopoly on basketball recruiting information. This is a first-class, first-rate operation and the last word for basketball recruiting in the nation. Bob is the most widely quoted "guru" regarding his sport than any other recruiting service in the U.S.

*****

BRUCE GRAHAM

Name of Service: *Crimson Times*

Address: P. O. Box 380966, Birmingham, Alabama 35238

Phone & Fax numbers: (205) 980-0660, (205) 980-8803 fax; additional number for Graham—(205) 323-7400

Publications: Bruce Graham is the managing editor of the *Crimson Times,* a specialty publication that heavily emphasizes recruiting in the state of Alabama. Bruce's work probably could be classified in the specialty publication section of this book, but he stresses recruiting so much that it can easily be considered a recruiting publication. A subscription costs $40. for 34 issues per year. *Crimson Times* obviously devotes much space to the University of Alabama athletics, but the recruiting scope is wide.

Ratings System: NONE

900 number: 900 number pending

Background: Bruce Graham combines radio and the print media to follow recruiting. Bruce has dabbled with his own recruiting service from time to time and has published several versions of newsletters. During the critical recruiting time periods, Bruce has added his expertise and his printed words to the pages of the *Birmingham Post-Herald* and the *Montgomery Advertiser.* Bruce has been following recruiting since 1984, when the big recruiting publication explosion occurred. He produces a radio call-in show for station WAPI and host Paul Finebaum in Birmingham. (See radio call-in show directory for further information).

Comments: Given a stable enterprise and format, Bruce Graham can crank out the necessary work for a solid recruiting service. His emphasis on Alabama recruits is limiting, but his information is solid. Bruce's biggest asset is that he is extremely versatile. Alabama fans surely would want to check out Bruce's efforts along with 'BAMA magazine which is published by Kirk McNair. (See specialty publications directory.)

*****

KEN GREENBERG AND JERRY SCARBROUGH

Name of Service: *The National Recruiting Advisor*

Address: P. O. Box 26825, Austin, Texas 78755-0825

Phone & Fax numbers: (713) 665-7383 or (512) 453-7995, (713) 665-5450

Publications: The *National Recruiting Advisor* comes in magazine and newsletter format. The July newsletter previews the top 100 players in the nation (cost: $5.). The *Advisor's* preseason magazine is published in August and this issue includes profiles and photos of top national recruits (cost: $15.). An updated top 200 players in the nation list comes out in newsletter form in October (cost: $5.). Top 10 players at each position are presented in a November newsletter (cost: $5.). The top players and their official or unofficial visits are the highlight of the December newsletter (cost: $10.). Commitments and visit updates are featured in the January newsletter (cost: $5.). The *Recruiting in Review* magazine is released in March after Signing Day and wraps up the top 50 recruiting classes. (cost: $15.). Total cost of the entire newsletter/magazine package is $55. with special discounts at certain times of the year. Additional newsletters issued in October cover the top 200 players in the Southeast, Southwest, plus the top 300 players in the Big 8 and Pac 10 conferences (cost: $10. each). Sneak previews in May are also featured as a bonus to the package. Credit cards are accepted.

900 number: 1-900-933-7776 at $1.95 for first minute and .95 cents for each additional minute.

Background: Ken Greenberg and Jerry Scarbrough are the publishers for this new service that originated in 1993. Ken Greenberg is a graduate of Oklahoma State and a longtime recruiting enthusiast from Austin, Texas. Prior to helping start up the *Advisor*, Ken was a successful computer salesman. Jerry Scarbrough is the former sports editor of the University of Texas student newspaper and he was a reporter for eighteen years for the Associated Press. Jerry currently publishes a specialty publication covering the University of Texas. Robert Williams, former chief talent scout for Max Emfinger, is the editor and scouting coordinator of the *Advisor*. Bobby Burton, Jr. is a film analyst and talent scout for the service. Greenberg and Scarbrough detail their reasons for publishing the *Advisor* as follows: "The *National Recruiting Advisor* is a new national recruiting service that was created...on the premise that serious recruiting fans deserve a serious news service that provides two commodities that are in short supply in this business—timely information delivered on schedule and accurate, up-to-date inside recruiting news." The first issue of the magazine also proclaims that the service will personally contact either the coach or the player for the recuriting inside information and provide all lists of official visits. Greenberg and Scarbrough promise that no information in the *Advisor* is more than four weeks old and they indicate that this particular service was started in response to the swirl ofinaccurate and umtimely information that frequently surfaces during the recruiting season. Again, in their printed words: "Too much of what passes for recruiting news is just gossip and secone-hand information that is months out of date even when it is reasonably accurate." Thus, the *National Recruiting Advisor* was formed.

Comments: This could be an up-and-coming operation to watch over the next several years. Greenberg and Scarbrough bring strong journalistic ability into the recruiting service reporting business. Robert Williams is an experienced recruiting service veteran, having performed much of the "down-and-dirty" work for Max Emfinger in Houston, Texas. The professional atmosphere of the service will be a plus. Greenberg and Scarbrough indicated that they want to provide recruiting enthusiasts with information that is professional, timely, accurate, and *unbiased.* Keep an eye on this service as it develops. The price is nice and they are getting off to a solid start with a good staff.

*****

PHIL GROSZ and TOM WEBER

Name of Service: *G & W Recruiting Report*

Address: P.O. Box 2021, Sanatoga, Pennsylvania 19464, or 97 Skytop Lane, Port Matilda, Pennsylvania 16870

Phone & Fax numbers: (814) 234-1177, (814) 231-2160 fax

Publications: *G & W Recruiting Report* is published in both newsletter and magazine form. There are six reports during recruiting season and an 80-page preseason magazine printed in August. Newsletters are mailed in December, mid-January, late January, February, March and a final 16-page report of all Division IA teams (107 listings). The subscription rate is $25. plus $5. for the preseason Top 250 players list published the last week in June.

Ratings System: *G & W* did not have a ratings system until 1992-93, when the service created its Top 250 list. The Top 250 is composed of team ratings based on the quality of players recruited plus how the teams met their recruiting needs. The service also rates the top 25 players at each position nationwide.

900 number: 1-900-454-3GNW or 1-900-454-3468 at $1.49 per minute. The *G & W* 900 number features eight phone lines with 64 possible selections. Each football conference and all independents are represented on the 900 number.

Background: In the shadows of Penn State at State College in Pennsylvania, Phil Grosz and Tom Weber print the *G & W* recruiting report. The service is affiliated with *Blue & White Illustrated*, a magazine devoted to the Penn State Nittany Lions (address: P.O. Box 1272, State College, Pennsylvania 16804). Phil and Tom follow recruiting nationally and concentrate on all areas of the country.

Comments: This service has been around for quite some time and is expanding. This is an inexpensive service. You won't find fancy photos or glitzy publications, just good ol' fashioned recruiting news in newsletter form. The reports are comprehensive and list all commitments by school, which is an excellent feature. A small, nationally advertised service for a very reasonable price.

*****

MAX HOWELL

Name of Service: Inside Sports Publications

Address: P. O. Box 566668, Atlanta, Georgia 31156

Phone & Fax numbers: 1-800-747-8879 for subscription information and 1-800-854-7654 for prospect information.

Publications: *Max Howell's Recruiting Guide* is a semi-national magazine geared towards the following states: Oklahoma, Texas, Louisiana, Arkansas, Mississippi, Alabama, Georgia, Florida, South Carolina, Tennessee, Pennsylvania, Michigan, and Ohio. A one-year subscription of six issues costs $39.95 per state. The guides are published in September, October, November, December, January, February, March, and May. The May issue previews upcoming recruits for the next Signing Day. Subscriptions last a calendar year beginning with the month the subscription is started. Capsules of each state listed are provided regarding high school and JUCO players. Each guide features articles and information from Max and local writers. Credit cards are accepted for payment of the guides. For a complimentary issue, you need only write the above address and request an issue. Max also offers a JUCO informational service available only to college coaches and programs and not for the general public's use or sale.

122

This JUCO guide is entitled *The National Junior College Football Recruiting Guide* and has a total of four issues costing $750. This guide is copyrighted and Max's service is currently utilized by 40 colleges and universities.

Ratings System: Max does not use numerical or star ratings systems. He lists all players alphabetically and then indicates their college choices. Max includes a quick bio sketch on top players and informational tidbits under each player's name. Max does name Al-l American teams in the JUCO ranks and places high school players in tiers with top recruits being rated higher than the Best of the Rest category.

900 number: 1-900-407-0000 at $1.49 per minute. Information updated daily and you must be 18 to call.

Background: Max Howell is a veteran of recruiting wars and knows the business inside and out. His knowledge of the JUCO system and teams is nationally renowned and acclaimed. Despite his years of experience, Max is still a "novice" as a recruiting "guru." Max started his current services in fall, 1991, when he teamed up with Forrest Davis and Mike Gordon, business manager of the *Ole Miss Spirit*. He recently expanded and moved his operations to Atlanta, Georgia. Max is a native of Alabama, having graduated from Autauga County High School.

After spending three seasons at Auburn on the football squad, Max transferred to Troy State, where he earned his undergraduate degree. As a member of the Trojans, Max received Little All-America honors. Upon graduation, he entered the high school ranks in Alabama. Max then returned to Auburn for his M.S. degree and he has completed doctoral work in Athletic Administration from Auburn and later at Florida State. In 1966, Max returned to Troy State for a stint as an assistant football coach. The Trojans compiled a record of 40-11-1 record from 1966 to 1970 during Max's term as Troy State assistant. The Trojans won four conference titles in this time period and the 1968 team claimed an NCAA Division II National Championship. The Troy State squads were built almost exclusively with top flight JUCO players under Max's recruiting guidance.

In 1970, Max left the coaching profession, but stayed at Troy State as an instructor for one year. Max then re-entered coaching on the high school level when he took over the high school head mentor slot at Niceville High in Niceville, Florida, in 1980. From Niceville, Max became head coach at Gulf Breeze High from 1982 through 1985. He then went to football power Escambia High in Pensacola, where he personally coached Emmitt Smith, one of the greatest high school running backs in Florida prep history. Emmitt would star at Florida and then sign with the Dallas Cowboys on completion of his junior year at Gainesvile.

Max left Escambia in 1987 when he took the position as strength coach at Pensacola Junior College. From there, Max joined Bobby Bowden's Florida State staff where he was the assistant recruiting coordinator and assistant secondary coach for the Seminoles. In 1988, Florida State finished 11-1 and third in the nation. During Max's term at Florida State, the Seminoles had No. 1 ranked recruiting classes by most recruiting service polls from 1988 to 1989.

Ole Miss hired Max as recruiting coordinator and administrative assistant to the athletic director in January, 1989, where he would serve until 1991. At Ole Miss, Max guided recruiting efforts that led the Rebels highly ranked recruiting classes. The Rebels were rated in the Top 10 by most recruiting services for 1989-1990 and 1990-1991 player classes. Ole Miss was ranked as having the No. 2 recruiting class in the SEC in 1990.

Max then returned to his old alma mater, Troy State, where he assumed the job of athletic director. Max directed evaluations and signings of 11 JUCO players to help the Trojans switch from Division II to Division IAA.

In fall, 1991, Max left Troy State to pursue his dream of a new JUCO recruiting service. Max soon formulated the *National Junior College Recruiting Guide* exclusively for college coaches. Max has been associated with the following standout players: Sim Byrd, 1968 All-American at Troy State; Vince Green, 1969 All-American at Troy State; Greg Wright, 1970 All-American at Troy State; Ronnie Shelby, 1970 All-American at Troy State; Emmitt Smith, who Max personally coached at Escambia, Florida, High School in 1986, became an All-American running back at Florida and went on to be the 1990 NFL MVP with the Dallas Cowboys; Deion Sanders, recruited by Max to Florida State who became an All-American and two sport star with the Atlanta Falcons and Atlanta Braves; and Randy Baldwin, an All-SEC running back with Ole Miss from 1989-1990, who was recruited by

Max from the JUCO ranks at Holmes Community College in Mississippi and went on to the NFL with the Minnesota Vikings and Cleveland Browns. Max has been involved with five NFL round one draft choices: RB Emmitt Smith with the Dallas Cowboys, DB/KR Deion Sanders with the Atlanta Falcons, DB Dexter Carter with the San Francisco 49ers who is out of Florida State, LB/DL Tony "Gator" Bennett out of Ole Miss who is now with the Green Bay Packers and DL Kelvin Pritchett out of Ole Miss, who was drafted originally, by the Dallas Cowboys and traded over to the Detroit Lions on draft day.

Comments: It's easy to say that nobody knows JUCOs like Max Howell knows JUCOs. Max is the foremost authority on building programs with JUCOs. His actual experience as a recruiting coordinator may give him an edge over his service competition.

*****

FREDDIE KIRBY AND BARRY HOLLAND

Name of Service: *Pigskin Preps*
Address: 369 Gordon Drive, Suite 17, Moulton, Alabama 35650
Phone & Fax numbers: (205)-974-5219 (no fax number)
Publications: *Pigskin Preps* is a newsletter service that emphasizes football recruits in the South only. Service costs $30 per year and includes eight newsletters and two magazines. The magazines are the preseason lists and the post-Signing Day review. Preseason magazine is a reference guide and 400 to 500 players are profiled in each newsletter.

Ratings system: Numerical based on positions. A 1 means a player can start as a freshman, 2 a sophomore, 3 a junior and, a 4 for players who can play when they become seniors.

900 number: NONE

Background: Freddie Kirby and Barry Holland are recruiting buffs who followed the signing season as a hobby. They started *Pigskin Preps* as an alternative to other services in 1991. They have worked with college coaches and film high school players on occasion.

Comments: *Pigskin Preps* is a very new service that comes highly endorsed, especially by Bill King, a recruiting heavyweight with WLAC, 1510 AM, out of Nashville, Tennessee. The price is certainly reasonable.

PHIL KORNBLUT

Name of Service: *The Recruiting News*

Address: South Carolina Network, 3710 Landmark Drive, Suite 100, Columbia, South Carolina 29204-4034 or P. O. Box 23592, Columbia, South Carolina 29224

Phone & Fax numbers: (803) 790-4305, (803) 790-4309 fax

Publications: *The Recruiting News is* published monthly during the months of June, July and August. The newsletter is published every two weeks during the recruiting months. Total package of 22 issues per year costs $40. Cost per issue is $2. The newsletter includes photos, interviews of top players, and roundups of football, basketball, and baseball recruiting news.

Ratings System: No internal rankings or ratings, but Phil does reprint or republish top lists from Max Emfinger, *G&W, Basketball Weekly, Basketball Times* and *The Poop Sheet.*

900 Number: 1-900-370-PREP or 1-900-370-7737 and the cost is $1.79 per minute. The 900 number includes breakdowns on all of the SEC teams and Clemson and covers South Carolina recruits in football and basketball.

Background: Since 1979, Phil Kornblut has been a sportscaster and is on the broadcasting team for the South Carolina Gamecocks through the South Carolina Network. Phil began following the recruiting wars in 1981 as an offshoot of his sportscasting. He also hosts a sports call-in show that is extremely popular in South Carolina, especially around the Columbia area. In 1984, a friend suggested that Phil start his newsletter due to the time he was spending on recruiting. Phil is considered the expert on South Carolina recruits and many other services, sportswriters, and sportscasters turn to Phil for his expertise. He also contributes a fine recruiting column to the *Spurs & Feathers* specialty magazine devoted to South Carolina. (See specialty publications directory for further information.)

Comments: If you want to know about what's happening in South Carolina, get in touch with Phil. A good service with excellent reporting and solid writing. Phil's articles that appear in *Spurs & Feathers* are must reading for Gamecock fans. This guy knows his way around the recruiting wars and has great contacts in the Carolinas and immediate recruiting areas.

TOM LEMMING

Name of Service: *Tom Lemming's Prep Football Report*
Address: 1104 East Point, Schaumburg, Illinois 60193
Phone & Fax numbers: (708) 893-8487, fax on request
Publications: *Tom Lemming's Prep Football Report* which is
published in July, August, September, November, January, and March.
The cost for the magazine is $50 annually and a fax service is available
for his newsletter. The magazine is an excellent production and
includes photos and ratings of each player broken down by specific
regions across the country.

Ratings System: Tom describes his rating system as a combination
of things based on player size, speed, potential, grades, college interest
in a player, and his own evaluations. Tom indicates that he personally
sees 90 percent of the nation's Top 500 players.

900 number: 1-900-860-9888 at $1.49 and subject to change as
Tom does not normally operate a 900 number. Menu is based on
favorite team selection. 1992-93 marked the first time Tom used a 900
number and the favorite team listings are produced by Tom with his
evaluations.

Background: Tom Lemming wrote for a local paper in the Chicago suburbs in the late 1970s when he began examining local recruiting. In 1977, Tom made plans for his own paper and in 1979, Tom
started his service, making him one of the creators of this business.
Tom's initial efforts centered on the Chicago area and expanded to the
midwest recruits in 1980. His service went nationwide in 1983, when
the recruiting service "explosion" began. Despite being slightly
handicapped by location, Tom has an excellent reputation. He takes a
"hands-on" attitude in dealing with players and coaches. Tom is a
frequent guest on the sports call-in show circuit, especially in December, January, and February—the prime recruiting months for football.
His service concentrates on high school players and does not normally
deal with JUCOs. The magazine format he uses is preferred by
subscribers and numerous sportswriters on the high school beat use
Tom's service to get a head start on preseason lists and postseason
honors.

Comments: Tom Lemming is another of the pioneers of this business and Tom is highly respected in the recruiting service circles. His magazine format is excellent and he is one of the first services to offer fax updates. While sometimes distant from southern and western states, Tom's concentration on the top players is admirable. He offers a good service at a reasonable price.

*****

JOE TERRANOVA

Name of Service: *Joe Terranova's Recruiting Reports*
Address: 3420 Eastham, Dearborn, Michigan 48120
Phone & Fax numbers: (313) 271-8024, no fax available
Publications: *Joe Terranova's Recruiting Reports* are published three times a year. A post-Signing Day edition is printed and released in mid-April. Top seniors are outlined in the early fall edition of the magazine. No newsletter or fax format is available. Both football and basketball recruits are covered in the reports. A "Total Package" subscription costs $30.

Ratings System: The original Terranova rating system rates recruits from four stars (****)—the top recruits—down to one star (*), the lower-rated recruits.

900 number: NONE and none contemplated in the future.

Background: Joe Terranova is the "Father of Recruiting Services." In charge of a training and communications department of the Ford Motor Company in Dearborn, Joe turned his hobby into the start of something big—for everyone else! Incredibly, Joe Terranova has been writing his magazine since 1970, which is the earliest known true recruiting service in the nation. For over 2 decades, the name of Joe Terranova has been immediately linked to recruiting services. Some may claim to have had the first services, but Joe is undeniably the Ancient Mariner of Recruiting. The publicity and success that Joe created and generated spread around the nation and Joe soon became the inspiration and framework for many recruiting services in existence today. It is no secret that many early recruiting services copied Joe's format and style before refining and redeveloping the systems. For Joe, his service is not a business, but a "labor of love." Joe is totally dedicated to Ford Motor Company and his hobby, which is his service.

It is because of his dedication to work that Joe does not devote full time to newsletters and 900 numbers. After all, Joe is a recruiting icon

128

and can afford to sit back and have fun. His free time during football and basketball recruiting is spent entirely on the phone tracking the whereabouts and whims of prospects across the land. His operation can't be described as a "Mom and Pop" organization since "Mom" (Joe's wife Karen) doesn't participate in any other way except for answering the phone. While other services passed him by and went for full-time dollars, Joe's service has remained calm, cool, and collected and a part of Joe's own perspective. In fact, Joe gave up radio call-in show appearances and the recruiting mainline publicity circuit several years ago because it took too time much away from his "real job." To Joe Terranova, following recruiting is pure fun—an outlet. No profit motive in the world drives Joe in his service and Joe has no regrets that he has not taken his ground-breaking business to a higher level. The familiar smiling football with a No. 1 symbol pointed in the air is truly symbolic of what Joe Terranova wishes his service to represent.

Comments: How do you comment about a legend? They say that other services have long since passed him by and that his service is outdated. You won't find any fancy photos, player films, 900 numbers, glitzy fax services and coffee table magazines, or any of the other extras that other services crank out for the dollars. But how many of those services can claim that they have been a trailblazing enterprise for over two decades? All other recruiting services listed in this book and those that appear in the future owe Joe Terranova an unpayable debt. Joe made recruiting fanatics fashionable and he is the Original Recruiting Guru—the first to make national exposure. "Joe The First" is still going strong!

*****

ALLEN WALLACE

Name of Service: *SuperPrep* Magazine

Address: P. O. Box 487, Laguna Beach, California 92652 (JCW Publishing)

Phone & Fax numbers: (714) 494-7866, (714) 497-3173 fax

Publications: *SuperPrep* magazine, which is a high-gloss magazine devoted to recruiting and high school players. A subscription includes three issues: a Pre-Season August issue, a Pre-Signing January issue, and a Letter-of-Intent March issue. The cost of *SuperPrep* is $59 per year and California residents must add $4.57

taxes (a total of $63.57 for California subscribers). A fax service called "SuperFax" is available for $79 and includes 23 fax recruiting reports which start in late November and run through Signing Day in February. SuperPrep and "SuperFax" combined are $138. (California folks pay $142.57). All faxes are transmitted in late evenings. Credit cards are accepted and prompt refunds are given if a subscriber is not satisfied.

Ratings System: Ratings in *SuperPrep* are comprised entirely of college coaches' recommendations.

900 number: Two numbers: 1-900-860-8500 and 1-900-740-7737 at $1.49 per minute. These numbers contain year round information and Allen described the menus for this service to be "floating menus." The format for the information flow changes on an "as-needed" basis.

Background: Allen Wallace bills his service as the "Rolls Royce of Recruiting." Allen is an attorney from California who wanted a publication a notch above the newsletters that were circulating in the early 1980s. He started *SuperPrep* in 1985 along with his brother, David Wallace. Allen and David believed that there was a void in the market and they decided to publish a color coffee-table-style magazine that featured players in great detail rather than mere listings. Allen and brother David advertise heavily and hire writers from different regions of the country to contribute to the service. Allen and David were able to put together their service very quickly. SuperFax was created in 1990 and he established his 900 service in late 1990. Allen's creative and glitzy ads utilize slogans such as "TGIF"—Thank God It's Football. One of *SuperPrep's* lifetime subscriber made the following statement: "All I want out of the divorce settlement is the *SuperPrep* subscription!"

Comments: *SuperPrep* lives up to its billing as being the "Rolls Royce of Recruiting" and the magazine is slickly produced and very complete. The price, however, is the "Porsche Price of Recruiting Services." It is expensive, but many subscribers swear by the magazine and utilize the services. Three issues for $60 makes it $20 per magazine and that is one of the higher-priced items. The SuperFax is a better bargain at $3 per faxed update. That's a good buy considering the cost of long distance phone calls and information gathering. Allen is one of the more highly respected recruiting "gurus" around. His regional reporting is solid, his color photos and features are, pardon the pun, "super," and it is obvious that he has given lots of thought and trial and error to his format. Allen is a frequent radio call-in show guest and quoted frequently by sportswriters during recruiting season and he always delivers. He provides profiles on recruits to numerous magazines, including *The Sporting News*. A good service at a higher-than-average price, but if you want a Rolls Royce, you have to pay Rolls Royce prices!

*****

JEFF WHITAKER

Name of Service: Southeastern Sports Publishing
Address: 1208-A Gunter Avenue, Guntersville, Alabama 35976
Phone & Fax numbers: (205) 582-5257, (205) 582-5680 fax & 1-800-239-9090
Publications: *Jeff Whitaker's Deep South Football Recruiting Guide*, which is a recruiting magazine released annually in late December and sold separately on newsstands for $3.95 per copy. The *Alabama/Auburn Football Preview* is a specialty annual previewing Alabama and Auburn football and is available for $3 in early June. Recruiting newsletter is entitled *Jeff Whitaker's Deep South Football Recruiting News* and is published monthly from August through April with two issues published in January for recruiting season. The subscription price for 10 issues of the newsletter is $24.95 per year. Jeff's services concentrate on high school and prep recruits and do not include JUCOs.

Ratings System: Jeff uses a numerical system. He states that "any rating system used to rate human potential is bound to be inadequate." That's a very accurate statement, but Jeff continues by saying "everyone in this recruiting business has to have one (ratings system) and the system we have works well for us." Jeff rates the Superstar recruits who can possibly be a four-year starter as a 10, a major college star and a possible three-year starter as a 9.50, a major college player and possible two- year starter as a 9.00 and a player with major college potential and a possible one-year starter as an 8.50 player. Jeff explains that his service uses a number of methods to determine these numbers. He indicates that since it is impossible to see every prospect play or even evaluate film on every player, he likes to speak to someone who has seen a player in person. Jeff then talks to writers who contribute to his annual magazine plus sportswriters in a prospect's area. Jeff employs a system which involves interviewing the opposing coaches who must go against top prospects. He says that an opposing coach is one of the best sources since he has no reason to sell you on a player who doesn't play for him. Jeff's experience with opposing coaches reveals that the coaches are usually very honest and the information they provide is very useful. Early in the recruiting season, when the opposing coaches have little time to talk, Jeff gathers information from college recruiting coordinators. Their evaluation of players is used by Jeff for his ratings system. Jeff sums up his system by adding that the best overall approach he takes is to have multiple opinions on each player. The more information from a prospect's recruiting questionnaire, his coach, the opposing coach, or a college recruiter, then the better prepared the service will be when it comes time to assign the ratings.

900 number: 1-900-740-2010 at $1.49 per minute. This number operates only in the months of December, January, and February and is subject to change.

Background: Jeff Whitaker created his service out of frustration in the early 1990s. He subscribed to many of the other services and found them to be too expensive, despite the wealth of information. Jeff has a background in radio broadcasting and banking and that rare mix has led to a tidy service. Jeff complained that the lower-priced services did not provide much information and were not worth the money. Jeff's goal is to be the best in terms of quality and quantity—a nice combination. His service is strictly designed as a middle-of-the-road recruiting service. By talking mainly to opposing coaches of recruits, he has opened up a new brand of rating system.

Comments: If you are looking for a nice economical recruiting service specializing in the south and southeastern region, then Jeff's annual and newsletter is just right for subscribers and recruiting nuts. The annual is perfect for the casual recruiting follower and the newsstand distribution is ideal. The only drawback of any newsstand annual is that once it is published (most of them hit the stands in mid-December or early January), the information in them about college choices is stale or completely outdated. Still, Jeff has a great service and he is always looking to improve it. It is a great "Bang for the

132

Bucks" service. This is a young aggressive service with a very bright future.

*****

JUCO SPECIALTY PUBLICATIONS

Name of Service: *JC Gridwire*

Address: P. O. Box 11703, Santa Ana, California 92711-1703

Phone & Fax numbers: (714) 997-0824, (714) 639-1532 fax

Publications: *JC Gridwire* is a newsletter/magazine format devoted entirely to the coverage of junior and community college players and their programs. There are 14 issues of *JC Gridwire* that run from the first week of September. The magazine offers the following: weekly Top 20 rankings, the annual All-American team, preseason roundup of all conferences, the annual Scholar-Athlete All-American sponsored by the NFL's Seattle Seahawks, the all-time statistical leaders in all important categories, a list of all coaches with 100 career wins plus those with outstanding winning percentages, annual preseason All-American team, special page each week highlighting the outstanding performances of individual players, general data on JUCO football plus coaching changes, conference realignments, flashbacks on previous All-American teams, All-Time teams, All-NFL teams, previous champs, editorials, plus bowl and playoff results. The total cost of a subscription is $35.

Ratings System: NONE

900 number: NONE

Background: Hank Ives is the editor/publisher of *JC Gridwire* and has been covering the JUCO scene for an incredible three decades plus since 1961. His magazine provides general information about JUCO football programs and the top players. Hank's location in California enables him to keep close watch on the numerous California JUCO programs and he takes the pulse of the Texas and Mississippi programs regularly. Hank bills *JC Gridwire* as the magazine that has "Everything you should know about community college football."

Comments: This is an excellent service for those fans who concentrate on JUCO players and signees. Hank has been doing this service a lot longer than any recruiting guru and that includes Joe Terranova, who started in 1970. No high school players, naturally, are featured. This publication is all JUCO and a great one at that!

SPECIALTY PUBLICATIONS

(in alphabetical order)
*****

'BAMA MAGAZINE

Name of Publication: *'BAMA Magazine*
Address: P. O. Box 6104, Tuscaloosa, Alabama 35486 or 2116 8th Street, Tuscaloosa, Alabama 34501
Phone & Fax numbers: (205) 345-5074, (205) 345-1260 fax
Subscription & Publishing Info: *'BAMA Magazine* is devoted to the University of Alabama athletic department activities and is printed monthly from August to May. In addition, *'BAMA* issues 14 newsletters, one after each football game and then on an "as-needed" basis. Price is $35 per year for a subscription with $10 additional overseas; Alabama residents must add $2 sales tax. Editor Kirk McNair is a former sports reporter. Kirk was assistant sports editor at the *Birmingham Post-Herald* from 1967-1970. He was sports information director at Alabama from 1973-1978. He created *'BAMA* magazine in fall, 1979, and started recruiting coverage that year. As far as Kirk's research can determine, no other specialty publication had touched on recruiting prior to *'BAMA*. Kirk describes starting the recruiting coverage in 1979 as "creating a monster."
900 number: 1-900-860-1979 with $2 for the first minute and $1 for each additional minute. Recruiting is updated weekly and then daily from January through Signing Day.
Comments: Kirk is an "old hand" in the recruiting wars. His specialty publication is one of the more widely read and one of the first of its type.
*****

BLUE & GOLD ILLUSTRATED

Name of Publication: *Blue & Gold Illustrated*
Address: P. O. Box 1007, Notre Dame, Indiana 46556
Phone & Fax number: (219) 277-6332
Subscription & Publishing Info: *Blue & Gold Illustrated* reports on the Fighting Irish of Notre Dame. The tabloid is published 20 times

a year—weekly during football and monthly during the off season. The magazine has a claimed circulation of over 150,000 readers. Free sample issues are available before ordering. A subscription is priced at $34.95, add $12 for first class during the football season for a total of $46.95 or add $20 for first class delivery for all issues or a total of $54.95. Credit cards are accepted.

900 number: 1-900-860-4244 at $2 for the first minute and 99 cents for each additional minute. The number is updated daily all season.

Comments: National publication is required reading for Fighting Irish fans.

*****

CANESPORT

Name of Publication: *CaneSport*

Address: 111 N.W. 183 Street, Suite 403, Miami, Florida 33169

Phone & Fax numbers: Not available for subscriber information

Subscription & Publishing Info: 21 issues for $31.95 with the emphasis on the Miami Hurricanes athletics teams. Published weekly during the season and monthly in the summer. For first class delivery, add $13, or a total of $44.95.

900 number: 1-900-454-2263 at $1.99 for the first minute and 95 cents for each additional minute. Comments: *CaneSport* is a new publication devoted to Miami fanatics.

*****

CATS' PAUSE

Name of Publication: *Cats' Pause*

Address: P. O. Box 7297, Lexington, Kentucky 40502

Phone & Fax numbers: (606) 278-3474, (606) 278-3477 fax

Subscription & Publishing info: Oscar Combs and Mike Estep control *Cats' Pause* which is totally immersed in Kentucky Wildcat sports. Oscar can be credited with creating the first-ever widely recognized specialty publication in the nation as he came up with *Cats' Pause* out of frustration for more information on Kentucky basketball. Oscar just simply could not get enough info on the Wildcats hoopsters from the local newspapers and sports magazines, so he came up with his own magazine devoted entircly to the Lexington demi-gods of basketball and the occasional interest in other 'Cat sports endeavors. *Cats' Pause* can be obtained for $34.50 per year and a subscription includes 35 issues.

900 number: NONE, but a *Cats' Pause* 900 number is scheduled to be operational at the first of April, 1992, and will run year round. The 900 number will focus on Kentucky football and basketball recruits.

Comments: Oscar is one of the true originators of specialty publications in the U.S. *Cats' Pause* was the first of its type in the late 1970s and Oscar's publication is one of the most respected and copied services of them all. Despite occasional competition in his own back yard, Oscar has persevered and prevailed against all comers and is considered by many to be the top specialty publication for Kentucky athletics.

*****

DAWGS' BITE
Name of Publication: *Dawgs' Bite*
Address: P. O. Drawer 6327, Miss. State, Mississippi 39762
Phone & Fax numbers: (601) 325-8881, (601) 325-2563 fax
Subscription & Publishing Info: *Dawgs' Bite* is edited by Joe Dier, and the magazine is an in-house specialty publication that was absorbed by Mississippi State. As such, the magazine is not an independent source of news covering the Mississippi State Bulldogs. Subscription costs are $30 per year for a total of 40 issues.

900 number: NONE

Comments: Joe Dier is a sports information veteran of Mississippi State and edits a magazine that has gone from an independent publication to an in-house arrangement. The photographer and former editor of *Dawg's Bite* is David Murray. The magazine features a column by Bob Hartley, also a former longtime Bulldog S.I.D. who is a highly respected writer. The downside for the magazine is the fact that recruiting cannot be examined prior to Signing Day. New players are profiled only after they are signed.

*****

GATOR BAIT
Name of Publication: *Gator Bait*
Address: P. O. Box 14022, Gainesville, Florida 32604

136

Phone & Fax numbers: (904) 372-1215, (904) 371-9420 fax, 1-800-782-3216 for subscription information.

Subscription & Publishing Info: David Stirt is the editor of *Gator Bait*, which covers the University of Florida athletics exclusively. David is considered one of the giants in the specialty publication business and was right there with *Cats' Pause* of Kentucky and *Tiger Rag* of LSU in length of existence. David's other writers include Marty Cohen and Scott Gregory. Subscription cost is $40 for 32 issues plus a special preseason glossy magazine. For first class delivery, add $17 during the football season for a total price of $57; first class delivery for the entire year costs an additional $32 for a total of $72 for first class delivery for all 32 issues. Credit cards are accepted. David and his magazine also offer "Gator Fax", a special recruiting service. Subscribers to this service have Super Fax, Deluxe Fax, or Recruiting Fax to choose from. The large fax package costs $200 and includes 50 fax reports that are sent out weekly from mid-October through December and then daily from January 1 to Signing Day. A Signing Day recap is also included with the Gator Fax.

900 number: 1-900-884-1100 at $2 for the first minute and $1 for each additional minute.

Comments: David Stirt is an outspoken writer who often runs headlong into controversy. David is especially opinionated about the NCAA and frequently voices objections aimed towards the rules set in Mission, Kansas. He provides a fabulous service for Florida Gator fans and his recruiting fax services have become immensely popular. David is one of the true innovators of the specialty publications business and runs a first class, first rate service.

*****

HAWGS ILLUSTRATED

Name of Publication: *Hawgs Illustrated*

Address: 5200 South Yale Avenue, Tulsa, Oklahoma 74135 and P. O. Box 1605, Fayetteville, Arkansas 72701

Phone & Fax numbers: (918) 491-4000, (918) 491-4001 fax 1-800-341-1522 for subscription information

Subscription & Publishing Info: Clay Henry is the managing editor of *Hawgs Illustrated*, a slick magazine that covers the University of Arkansas Razorbacks athletics scene. Clay's enterprise is called College Sports Communications and also publishes *Sooners Illustrated* (Oklahoma), *Huskers Illustrated* (Nebraska), *Aggies Illustrated* (Texas A&M) ,and *Voice of the Hawkeye* (Iowa). *Hawgs Illustrated* is published 17 times a year with a subscription price tag of $39.90. Credit cards are accepted and subscription orders are processed by mail through the Fayetteville address listed.

College Sports Communications was formerly known as Sports Magazines of America, an operation that folded in the mid- to late 1970s. *Sooners Illustrated* was created in 1978 and *Huskers Illustrated* came out in 1981. *Hawgs Illustrated* began publication in April, 1992. Clay Henry is a veteran sportswriter/editor and spent 14 years with the *Tulsa World* before taking over *Hawgs Illustrated.* Clay's father was sports editor of the *Arkansas Gazette* for years and Clay is a solid Razorback. All sports are covered for Arkansas in the magazine with heavy emphasis on football and basketball. Clay reports that 25% of the magazine is devoted to football and basketball recruiting, especially in the Spring editions. *Hawgs Illustrated* has over 6,000 subscribers. Contributing writers to the magazine are veteran sportswriters including Wadie Moore of the *Pine Bluff Commercial*, Randy Crable of *Tulsa World* and James Hale out of Norman, Oklahoma.

900 number: 1-900-RUN-HAWG or 1-900-786-4294 at $1.99 for the first minute and .99 cents for each additional minute.

Comments: This is a bright new specialty publication with a solid publishing background and it has received a tremendous jump start with a large number of subscribers. Clay Henry is an outstanding follower of Arkansas with great contacts and his magazine is a must for Razorback fans.

*****

INSIDE THE AUBURN TIGERS

Name of Publication: *Inside the Auburn Tigers*
Address: P. O. Box 2666, Auburn, Alabama 36830
Phone & Fax numbers: (205) 745-4370, (205) 745-4653 fax
Subscription & Publishing Info: Mark Murphy is the editor of *Inside the Auburn Tigers*, which obviously covers the athletic goings-on at the Plains in Alabama. A subscription costs $30. and that includes 10 monthly magazines that go to print from August to May and 11 newsletters that are published and mailed weekly during the

football season. Mark is in his 12th year of editing *Inside the Auburn Tigers.*

900 number: 1-900-860-0123 at $2.00 for the first minute and $1 for each additional minute from touchtone or rotary phones. The AU Tiger Hotline is a 24-hour, seven-day-a-week operation providing information on Auburn University sports. Menu changes each May, but features football and basketball updates, scouting reports, and recruiting information. In the summer, monthly updates are available. During the fall, Mark updates weekly except during the early basketball signing period, when updates are daily. The number is updated three times a week during recruiting in January and February and immediate updates are provided for breaking news. The service is a natural expansion of the monthly magazine and weekly newsletter.

Comments: Mark Murphy follows the Auburn athletic scene closely and is very knowledgeable about recruiting. Mark's 900 number may be one of the most comprehensive of the specialty publications.

*****

THE OLE MISS SPIRIT

Name of Publication: *The Ole Miss Spirit*

Address: 128 Hillside Drive, Oxford, Mississippi 38655 for subscriptions; 1603 University Avenue, Oxford, Mississippi 38655 for letters to the editor and other mail

Phone & Fax numbers: 1-800-748-8528 or (601) 236-2263 (800 number used for fax)

Subscription & Publishing Info: Chuck Rounsaville is publisher and editor. *The Ole Miss Spirit* is published weekly during football and basketball seasons and twice monthly during spring sports. Total of 32 issues per year and total cost is $35 or $48 for first class mail subscription . The marketing director is Mike Gordon, SEC columnist is Stan Torgerson ;and recruiting columnist (The Back Page) is Glen Waddle. Other columnists include Jimmie McDowell, former executive director of the National Football Foundation and longtime sportswriter from Mississippi ,also known as "Mississippi Red."

900 number: 1-900-990-6477 at $1.95 for the first minute and 95 cents per minute for each additional minute. The 900 number is active from August until June.

Comments: Since 1982 *The Ole Miss Spirit* has covered the athletic scene of the University of Mississippi Athletic Department (Ole Miss). The *Spirit* pioneered the usage of 900 numbers in the late 1980s. Chuck Rounsaville originally was the editor of the *Spirit* and the former publisher and partner in the operation was Mac Gordon, who now writes in the business section of the Jackson, Miss. *Clarion Ledger*. Recruiting columnist Glen Waddle has written for the *Spirit* on the Back Page since 1984.

*****

OSCEOLA

Name of Publication: *Osceola*
Address: 402 Dunwoody Street, Tallahassee, Florida 32304
Phone & Fax numbers: Not available
Subscription & Publishing Info: Devoted to Florida State, *Osceola* is published 32 times a year for $38. First class mail service costs $56 total, an extra $18 for year-round delivery. Football season first class service costs an additional $10 or $48 total. Credit cards are accepted. *Osceola* is in its 12th year of publication.

900 number: 1-900-860-4378 at $2 for the first minute, and $1 for each additional minute.

Comments: A must for Seminole fans of all kinds.

*****

SPURS & FEATHERS

Name of Publication: *Spurs & Feathers*
Address: Box 8055, Columbia, South Carolina 29202
Phone & Fax number: (803) 256-1789, same number for fax
Subscription & Publishing Info: Dexter Hudson is the editor of *Spurs & Feathers* which reports on the University of South Carolina athletics. Phil Kornblut writes the recruiting column for *Spurs & Feathers* and is listed separately in this recruiting service index. The magazine is fairly new on the scene, but does a fantastic job of following the Gamecocks. A subscription costs $30 for 38 issues during the athletic year with a special preseason issue kicking things off in the summer.

900 number: 1-900-370-7737 (Phil Kornblut number) at $1.79 per minute covering all SEC schools and Clemson. There is no specific

900 number for *Spurs & Feathers*. The Kornblut number is not related directly to the magazine.

Comments: Excellent publication and good recruiting news. Dexter puts together a fine magazine with loads of info. The Kornblut column is a must for recruiting fans.

*****

TIGER RAG

Name of Publication: *Tiger Rag*

Address: P. O. Box 2305, Hammond, Louisiana 70404 for sugscription information; 2854 Kalurah Street, Baton Rouge, Louisiana 70808 for correspondence to the editor.

Phone & Fax numbers: (504) 343-4LSU (or 504-343-4578); (504) 343-1579

Subscription & Publishing Info: *The Tiger Rag* covers LSU athletics in 36 magazines published from August to June. Subscription price is $48. per year. Special issues are printed depending upon the athletic season and time of year. Raghead, Inc., is the publisher of *Tiger Rag* and the owner is George Solomon.

900 number: 1-900-896-1578 at $1.50 for the first minute and 75 cents for each additional minute .

Comments: *The Tiger Rag* is the second specialty publication of its kind to appear shortly after Oscar Combs created *Cats' Pause* for Kentucky enthusiasts in Lexington, Kentucky. *Tiger Rag* was founded on June 6, 1978, by Steve Myers, Steve Townsend and Gary Solomon. Baton Rouge native John Massey is the new editor of *Tiger Rag*. John spent much of his life just miles away from the LSU campus and he started his writing career with the Baton Rouge *Morning Advocate*. After spending 5 years at the *Advocate* covering every conceivable sporting event, John would move on to become sports editor for the next 3 years at daily newspapers in Abbeville, DeRidder and Sulphur, Louisiana. John then returned to Baton Rouge to work part time in the LSU sports information department while earning his college degree. Before assuming editorial control of *Tiger Rag* in 1993, John served as Associate Communications Director for the Sun Belt Athletic Conference. The assistant editor of the *Tiger Rag* is veteran J. R. Ball, who is one of the top recruiting writers in the South. Other regular *Tiger Rag* columnists include: Glenn Guilbeau of the Alexandria *Town Talk*;

Scooter Hobbs, who is sports editor of the Lake Charles *American Press*; Jimmy Hyams of the Knoxville, Tennessee, *News-Sentinel*; Jim Engster, who is sports director of the Louisiana Network which broadcasts LSU athletic events; and local businessman Allan Crow. *Tiger Rag* provides independent, objective coverage of all LSU athletics. A subscription to this established and well marketed magazine is a must for LSU fans, and the 900 number features a comprehensive menu.

*****

RADIO SPORTS CALL-IN SHOWS

(Stations listed are those considered most popular by recruiting fans across the south.)

ATLANTA, GEORGIA

Name of Station: WSB, 750 AM

Address: 1601 Peachtree Street, Atlanta, Georgia 30309

Phone & Fax numbers: (404) 897-7500, (404) 897-7363 fax, Call- in show number: (404) 872-0750

Call -in show format: *SportsTalk* on WSB in Atlanta airs Monday through Friday from 6-7 P.M. Eastern time and on Saturdays from 4-7 P.M. Eastern and on Sundays from 7-8 P.M.. Eastern. Longtime Georgia Bulldog play-by-play announcer Larry Munson, former Atlanta Falcon Jeff Van Note, and Bill Rosinski are the rotating hosts for *SportsTalk*. Recruiting guests are frequent during recruiting season and up to Signing Day. WSB has a 50,000 clear channel signal and also airs Atlanta Braves broadcasts.

900 number: NONE

Comments: *SportsTalk* is at its best during football season. Although it is not as well known for recruiting shows, the station features experienced hosts who schedule recruiting gurus and related guests.

*****

BATON ROUGE, LOUISIANA

Name of Station: WIBR, 1300 AM

Address: 1815 Lafiton Lane, Port Allen, Louisiana 70767

Phone & Fax numbers: (504) 344-2666 (office & fax no.) or (504) 387-1300 call-in show number.

Call-in show format: WIBR features an all sports format with national and local shows. Hosts for this popular station are: Jon Fine,

Bryan Rushing, Todd Black, Bruce Hunter, and Buddy Songy. The local shows air beginning at 7 A.M. and run until the early evening hours when the national shows take over. All hosts are well versed in football and basketball recruiting. Being located in Baton Rouge, LSU athletics are the frequent topics but the shows touches all bases when it comes to sports. Host Bruce Hunter is a former Baton Rouge *Morning Advocate* sports writer. Fine, Songy, and Rushing deal with recruiting on a regular basis. WIBR has a signal strength of 5,000 watts.

900 number: NONE

Comments: WIBR has emerged out of stout competition to become the no. 1 sports call-in show format in this sports laden area of Louisiana. Competitor WJBO airs LSU Tiger Talk, but WIBR now clearly owns the airwaves. In the last several years, the Baton Rouge market had as many as three stations with sports call-in formats, but WIBR has taken over completely and thoroughly. If the station ever increases its signal, this could become one of the top stations for recruiting in the south. It already draws a vast audience in Tiger Land at LSU and is recommended listening for anyone cruising through the area.

*****

BIRMINGHAM, ALABAMA

Name of Station: WERC, 960 AM

Address: 500 Beacon Parkway West, Birmingham, Alabama 35209

Phone & Fax numbers: (205) 942-9600, or (205) 945-9372 call-in show number.

Call-in show format: Matt Coulter and William Jenkins host this popular show on WERC in Birmingham from 4 to 7 P.M. on Monday through Friday. Recruiting is a major topic in January and February and Max Emfinger is a recruiting guest during this time period. Signal strength is 5000 watts.

900 number: NONE

Comments: Matt Coulter and his crew produce a solid call-in show involved in heavy competition in the Alabama area. This show battles toe-to-toe with the other shows.

*****

Name of Station: WJOX, 690 AM

Address: 236 Goodwin Crest Drive, Birmingham, Alabama 35209

Phone & Fax numbers: (205) 945-4646, (205) 942-8959 fax Call-in show numbers: (205) 942-6900 or 1-800-467-6900

Call-in show format: WJOX is a 24-hour all sports all the time station similar to WFAN in New York City. Doug Layton, former Alabama play-by-play announcer-hosts the morning version from 8 to 10 A.M. Ben Cook anchors the afternoon/evening show. The station signal strength is 50,000 watts during the day and reaches north and central Alabama.

900 number: NONE

Comments: The all sports format is a natural for call-in shows, but the format at this station floats from time to time. More stability as to times is needed before this format will be solidly in place. The station does have a solid sports lineup, as they are the flagship carrier for the Birmingham Bulls minor league hockey team and the Birmingham Barons minor league AA baseball team.

*****

Name of Station: WAPI, 1070 AM

Address: 2146 Highland Avenue South, Birmingham, Alabama 35205

Phone & Fax numbers: (205) 933-9274, (205) 933-6708 fax Call-in show numbers: (205) 741-9274

Call-in show format: Controversial host Paul Finebaum hosts the call-in show from 5 to 7 P.M. Mondays through Fridays. The show is produced by Bruce Graham, who is an occasional sportswriter for the *Birmingham Post Herald*. Bruce is also a noted recruiting expert as he follows Alabama recruiting quite closely.

900 number: NONE

Comments: The Finebaum show is the No. 1 rated show in a tough competitive market. Like him or hate him, most in Birmingham have to listen to him to get the latest.

*****

MEMPHIS, TENNESSEE

Name of Station: WMC, 790 AM

Address: 1960 Union Avenue, Memphis, Tennessee, 38119

Phone & Fax numbers: (901) 274-7979 for call-ins or (901) 274-7979 star (*) 79 toll free for Bell South Mobility customers or 1-800-759-6279

Call-in show format: Mike Fleming, former sportswriter for the

144

Memphis *Commercial Appeal,* hosts the top-rated show in the Memphis radio market covering the Mid-South areas of west Tennessee, Arkansas, and north Mississippi. The show airs Monday through Friday from 6:05 to 7:30 P.M. Mike brings in top guests and encourages a free wheeling call-in format. SportsTalk 79 emphasizes recruiting heavily in December and January. WMC is the carrier of Ole Miss football and basketball in the Memphis area.

900 number: NONE

Comments: Mike Fleming has brought his journalistic abilities to the radio airwaves to great success in Memphis. He is thorough in presentation and airs a very respected program. This is the top-rated show in Memphis and one of the better call-in shows in the South. The guests are timely, lively- and very topical.

*****

Name of Station: KIX, 560 AM

Address: 5900 Poplar Avenue, Memphis, Tennessee 38119

Phone & Fax numbers: (901) 767-6532, (901) 767-9531 fax
Call-in show numbers: (901) 535-9560

Call-in show format: George Lapides, a Memphis sports personality, hosts this show from 5:00 P.M. until 7:00 P.M. Monday through Friday. Lapides is a former sportswriter and the former general manager of the Memphis Chicks AA professional baseball team. KIX is the Memphis State flagship station and there is a strong emphasis towards Memphis State basketball and football.

900 number: NONE

Comments: This is a free-wheeling show that offers a lot of good natured talk. He has many contacts in sports in the Memphis area and produces a very competitive show.

*****

Name of Station: WREC, 600 AM .

Address: 203 Beale Street, Suite 200, Memphis, Tennessee 38103

Phone & Fax numbers: (901) 578-1160, (901) 525-8054 fax Call-in show numbers: (901) 535-9732

Call-in show format: Dave Woloshin produces a call-in show from 5 to 7 P.M. on weeknights. Woloshin is a newcomer to the Memphis area but brings with him a rich sports background. WREC is heavy on sports, as the station is the flagship carrier for the Memphis

Chicks AA baseball team and the Memphis River Kings, a minor league CHL hockey team. The station also airs Tennessee Volunteer football and basketball plus other shows related to Tennessee athletics. This is an up-and-coming show in the Memphis market.

900 number: NONE

Comments: Sports fans of all types will appreciate this station and its strong emphasis on its sports format. The call-in show is a natural lead-in for the baseball and hockey games. A strong station with a bright future in the sports call-in show ratings wars. The show features recruiting updates from someone named "Guru Gordon."

*****

MONTGOMERY, ALABAMA

Name of Station: WLWI, 740 AM

Address: P. O Box 4999, Montgomery, Alabama 36195

Phone & Fax numbers: (205) 945-4646, (205) 240-9219 fax Call-in show number: 1-800-239-9544

Call-in show format: Jim Fyffe, voice of the Auburn Tigers, and Bill Cameron host a nightly call-in show Monday through Friday from 4-6 P.M. Bill is one of the foremost recruiting followers in the South and the show has a heavy emphasis on recruiting. Guests such as Max Emfinger, Bruce Graham, and Forrest Davis are on frequently during the peak recruiting months. Jim is a veteran sportscaster and has been the play-by-play announcer for Auburn since 1981; he is a very reliable and very capable call-in show host. Recently, Jim networked this show across the state of Alabama and the show is now heard in Birmingham, Selma, Auburn-Opelika, and North Alabama in addition to the Montgomery area.

900 number: NONE

Comments: This is one of the best known and top call-in shows in the South. The recruiting information flows freely during recruiting and Jim and Bill insure that the guests reappear on the show to keep listeners listening and calling. Next to WLAC in Nashville, probably one of the best sources for recruiting information. A classy show with classy hosts.

*****

NASHVILLE, TENNESSEE

Name of Station: WLAC, 1510 AM

Address: 10 Music Circle East, Nashville, Tennessee 37203

Phone & Fax numbers: (615) 256-0555, (615) 242-4826 fax

Call-in show numbers: (615) 737-9522 or 1-800-688-WLAC

Call-in show format: Bob Bell and Bill King host one of the top sports call-in shows in the nation at WLAC. The show airs from 5 P.M. to 8 P.M. Monday through Saturdays. WLAC is a 50,000 clear channel station that is listened to by sports fans throughout the South. The conversation is lively and always topical. Bill King is recognized as one of the top recruiting reporters in the South. Bob Bell is a respected journalist who also works as a play-by-play announcer, and he is a former TV sports personality. This show is the shining beacon of all sports call-in shows with its only rival being that of sports-laden KMOX, 1120 AM in St. Louis.

900 number: 1-900-288-4546 at $1.49 per minute. Bill King provides all of the recruiting information on this line and it covers the SEC, selected ACC teams and other schools in the area. The number is exclusively a product of Bill King and his recruiting information.

Comments: If you're a recruiting junkie and a sports purist, this is the call-in show for you. It far and away outworks and outperforms any other call-in show in the South. No one puts more hours into the content of their show and the 900 number than Bob and Bill. The duo was formerly joined by Charlie McAlexander, the Vanderbilt play-by-play announcer who left in 1992 to join the Kentucky broadcasting teams in football and basketball. WLAC is the flagship station for Vanderbilt Commodore football and basketball games, which pre-empt Bob and Bill on occasion.

*****

NEW ORLEANS, LOUISIANA

Name of Station: WWL 870 AM, WSMB 1350 AM

Address: 1450 Poydras, Suite 440, New Orleans, Louisiana 70112

Phone & Fax numbers: (504) 593-6376 or (504) 593-2137, (504) 593-1850 fax

Call-in show format: Buddy Diliberto, longtime New Orleans sports personality, anchors the famed WWL sports call-in show from 6-8 P.M. daily in New Orleans. Buddy replaces the late legendary Hap

Glaudi, one of the most famous sports radio hosts in the nation. Larry Matson, another veteran sports reporter, also hosts the WWL show. Ken Trahan hosts the WSMB show from 4-6 P.M. daily. WWL has a major league 50,000 clear channel signal while WSMB has a signal strength of 5000 watts.

Comments: WWL has been the heart and soul for New Orleans and Louisiana sports fans for decades. LSU and Tulane fans either swear by or swear at the WWL coverage. WWL is also very heavy on New Orleans Saints coverage. WWL is the station where Max Emfinger first made his mark in the mid-1980s.

*****

ADDITIONAL SERVICES & MAGAZINES NOT REVIEWED

Jeff Weinburger, Memphis, Tennessee and/or Southaven, Mississippi. Jeff is a recruiting follower that has a 900 number service advertised on WLAC, 1510 AM in Nashville, Tennessee. No information is available as to newsletters and/or other services provided by Jeff. His 900 number listed is 1-900-370-PREP or 1-900-370-7737. When his ads are aired on WLAC, a strong disclaimer follows the ads indicating that the service is separate and independent. This is a call at your own risk situation. Other services not listed completely are as follows:

Southern Basketball Report, Bill Ellis, Clark Francis, Louisville, Kentucky

The Bulldog Magazine, P.O. Box 1472, Athens, Georgia/Jeff Hundley, Publisher; Phone No. (706) 542-3944

Host Communications, Inc., 120 Kentucky Avenue, Lexington, Kentucky 40505; Phone No. (606) 233-3455

Tom Hammond Productions, 2526 Regency Road, Lexington, Kentucky 40503; Phone No. (606) 278-8437

Volunteers Magazine, P.O. Box 47, Knoxville, Tennessee 37901, Tom Mattingly, Publisher; Phone No. (615) 974-1212

(Other publications devoted to University of Tennessee include: *Big Orange Illustrated & Rocky Top Views*.

Dean Augustin's Prep Sports News, 4101 Sonora Drive, Plano, Texas 75074, phone (voice mail) (214) 622-5173, 10 issues at $29.95, $99.95 for fax service, 900 number is 1-900-28-TEXAS at $1.49 per minute. (Service specializes in Texas high school prospects).

CHAPTER 10

Leftovers and
Leftouts

I
T WAS WRITTEN in this book that as soon a recruiting books
hit the presses, they are almost outdated. Every attempt has been
made to keep this reference book up to date and fresh. The survey
conducted by the author and the *Ole Miss Spirit* occurred over a one-
year peroid from June, 1992, through June, 1993. Every effort was
made to reach all of the recruiting services by mail, phone, or fax.

If there is a service, specialty publication, or call-in show that
focuses on recruiting which does not appear in this book, please write
or contact one of the following addresses:

> Glen Waddle
> 178 Travis Wood
> Jackson, Mississippi 39212
> Phone (601) 372-3422; Fax (601) 373-6624
> or
> Quail Ridge Press
> P.O. Box 123
> Brandon, Mississippi 39043
> Phone (601) 825-2063; Fax (601) 825-3091

As a final fling to this piece of work (well, some might call it that!),
be it known that recruiting services have recently been blamed by
college coaches for problems in contacting recruits. In the 1993
NCAA meetings, coaches openly complained that the rules calling for
one phone call to recruits per week was being compromised because of
recruiting gurus. The logic went like this: since the coaches could
only call once a week, they had to rely on recruiting services for
information and that these "gurus" were a "cancer of society."

Coaches were claiming that the gurus could call the recruits but they couldn't.

First, any coaching staff that relies solely on any of these services for recruiting information and to sign players should resign instantly. Second, this so-called "cancer of society" is a cottage industry of newsletters, 900 numbers, lists, and evaluations that exists on rumors, hearsay, and phone calls with players who can change their minds based on the color of a team's T-shirts!

Have you ever *Heard Anything* so ridiculous?

Index

.